Sex, Love, & the Spacetime Pinch

by

Vee Bentley

This is a work of fiction. Names, characters, places, and incidents are either the product of the author's imagination or are used fictitiously, and any resemblance to actual persons living or dead, business establishments, events, or locales, is entirely coincidental.

Sex, Love, & the Spacetime Pinch

Contact Information: info@thewildrosepress.com

The Wild Rose Press, Inc.
PO Box 708
Adams Basin, NY 14410-0708

Visit us at www.thewilderroses.com

Publishing History
First Scarlet Rose Edition, 2017
Digital ISBN 978-1-5092-1434-1
Trade Paperback ISBN 978-1-5092-3263-5

Published in the United States of America

Dedication

To my love and loving husband, through all my names!

To the Tucson RWA and to the GV Writers. My special thanks and a hug to critique partner Denise, who encouraged me to finish this book.

And to Melanie, Diana, and the other great editors at TWRP. It's a pleasure to work with you.

Part One
The First Expedition

Chapter One

How she wanted to pummel him! Pound away at that hard body, letting loose all her frustration. Lara could feel her fists drumming rat-a-tat against Tenn's massive chest. *Ha!* Pebbles thrown against a brick wall would have a greater impact.

No, responding physically wasn't an option. What can a five-foot-eight, one hundred thirty-pound female do to vent? The swear words she knew had grown flaccid from overuse, limp dicks drained of their power. She couldn't scream or, Space forbid, allow a tear to squeeze out of her eye. One spark of feminine reaction and she could wave goodbye to any chance of reversing the Navy's decision.

Ensign Lariana P. Stone refused to accept defeat. She may have dithered over her decision to act, but no one knew that. Her father and brothers would be furious to learn she broke rank, but the more she thought, the more she realized her only chance was to go over the captain's head. She might even approach the admiral!

Well, maybe not that high.

Captain Tenn James didn't want her on the mission, and she knew why. She looked fragile—small boned and slim—but looks were deceiving. She'd been well trained in hardship. Her body was toned. She survived all the obstacle courses the Naval Aerospace

Command devised. Watching her diet paid off, no excess weight to slow her down. And she aced both the written and the tactical exams. Yes, she was fit for the job, and she'd damn well see to it that his superiors knew it.

There, in classroom three of the windowless concrete block the Navy used for its procedural training sessions in space flight, hidden from the cloudless blue sky and endless sunshine of Catalina Island, Lara shut out all awareness of her family's negative response to her decision and concentrated on winning.

In the weeks that followed, using logic, persistence, and veiled threats of discrimination proceedings, Lara chipped away at the objections to her joining the mission. She faced negative comments with outstanding performance, never lost her cool, and no matter how tough the training, never bitched. When her name was finally announced as the third member of the crew, she turned away from Tenn's stoic expression to hide her smirk.

During the year in space they'd been given to find a habitable planet, Lara knew she could convince the captain she had been the right choice for the job. A necessary part of the team.

She'd be all business.

Never lose her temper.

Never let on that she was crazy about him.

Chapter Two

As the moonbeams dimmed, and the far-off light grew brighter in the sky, the stars along its path faded away. The object grew nearer, ejecting its streaming particles of ice. Sensing its approach, the planet quivered in anticipation.

A soft breeze sprang up, ruffling the cool waters of the lake. Wavelets lapped at the sandy shore. In the forest beyond, tree leaves fluttered, whispering to each other in a wordless language.

Then the wind stilled. And the hum beneath the quiet returned.

****

Eight months later…

"It must be autumn down there."

Lara peered out the spacecraft's silicone window at the planet below, her eyes adjusting to the dizzying descent. Rising up to meet the ship, a riot of reds and oranges, pinks and purples exploded in her vision. The foliage appeared to be Earthlike…and yet, somehow alien. From this distance, she couldn't guess why.

The shapes were familiar, the fall colors warm and inviting. A bit more purple than she was used to, but not enough to cause her unease. Perhaps it was the lack of green…

Through the screech of rotors punishing the atmosphere as they slowed the craft, Lara heard Tenn's voice in her headphones. "This planet looks promising. Hot colors. I smell passion."

"Might have known sex would be your first reaction," she teased. "You're so predictable, Tenn James."

"That's Captain James, nanopunk. Hey, I have to keep up my reputation. There's a patch of blue down there. Could be water, do you think? We may have lucked out."

"Hold your horses," Gordon cut in. The third member of the team was half a head shorter than the captain, built more like a tennis player who didn't practice often enough. "Don't get excited and go off half-cocked when we land. Give the computer a chance to check air compatibility and water safety."

"Do I ever go off half-cocked?" Tenn demanded. Lara's laughter came lilting through the headphones.

"Yeah, yeah, you're always fully cocked," Gordon replied. "My bad. Just be careful. We haven't had much experience with earthlike planets. So far, this mission has found only hostile atmospheres."

"We know," Lara insisted before the two men could start arguing again. Amazingly, instead of constantly being put down, she ended up being peacemaker throughout their voyage. An alpha male like Tenn—big, handsome, forceful, and impatient— was bound to irritate a dedicated scientific geek like Gordon from time to time. There had been lots of time on their long voyage, even with hyperspace jumping the light-years.

Lots of time, too, for her to squelch the shivers that slid inside her whenever she and the captain came into contact. Even bumping into his spacesuit aroused a tiny internal quake. Despite his attempt to exclude her from this mission, her desires hadn't diminished. If anything, frustration intensified them.

She now knew why he'd asked for a different crew. "Keeping Ensign Stone safe will be a distraction," he said. *Chauvinist male!* 'Superior' and 'SEAL' were words meant for each other, but she never said that aloud. This was her first real voyage in space. After the training missions, she knew that any attitude coming from her was unacceptable, and would ruin her career as well. She continued to play it cool. It paid off in a smooth-running, unemotional flight.

Most of the time. Well, except for the day they landed hard on an inhospitable planet. She unstrapped too soon and bumped into Gordon's arm, causing a wild reading on the computer. She smiled, remembering the new curse words she picked up that day. She hadn't known any in Chinese before and yes, they were inscrutable and hard to pronounce. She rolled her eyes at the memory.

"Guys, I'm thrilled to find a mini-planet that's not filled with ammonia," she said, "or isn't a moonscape of jagged rocks and dry dust. This one looks habitable. Maybe our mission will be a success after all—and we can go home."

At once, the atmosphere lightened. All it took was the mention of home. Amazing how well the three of them got along, once they were aboard. Especially considering the eight months together, all that time having to hide her feelings…

Good thing they each had a sense of humor. Well, at least she and Tenn laughed a lot. Gordon was so absorbed in his experiments he tracked differently. His obliviousness to innuendo was funny in itself. She'd never forget the puzzled look he gave her when she interrupted a nasty squabble with that great line from Oscar Wilde, "True friends stab you in the front." A minute passed before he came up with a weak, "Ha ha."

When he wasn't talking science, Gordon mooned about a lab tech named Akemi. After eight months, Lara felt she knew the girl, all five feet one inch of her. She could almost reach out and touch the shiny black braid that bounced on the girl's butt.

Yes, they made the best of a dull trip. Too bad she hadn't been able to pique the captain's interest, but that could change now. *Oh, yeah*. She ran her tongue around her lips.

"Ready for touchdown," Tenn called, checking that everyone was strapped in. "And hold the 'oof,' Lara."

"Can't…oof!" She grinned at him as the craft shuddered to a landing and air returned to her lungs.

Gordon was already at the computer checking the atmosphere. "Nitrogen and oxygen similar to Earth. Some trace elements the computer doesn't recognize yet, but the amount seems small enough to be safe. We've lucked out on gravitational force, too. It's almost identical to Earth's. The most you'll feel is a little more spring in your steps, and there must be active hotspots beneath the planet's surface, because the air is warm, even this far from its sun. The computer's registering a sub-tropical climate."

Lara could smell Tenn's impatience. She shivered as it resonated with hers.

"Okay, it's giving the all clear, though it's still analyzing," Gordon said. "You two go ahead. I'll keep gathering the facts. Stay in sight." He looked directly at

Lara.

"We know the drill, Lieutenant Lee." She patted his shoulder with her gloved hand. Sometimes she felt her brothers had sneaked aboard the ship. This protective bit was a pain in the ass.

Tenn swept the touch pad. The door unlocked, a ladder descended, and he and Lara climbed down. They tested the air carefully, and then lifted the transparent visors on their helmets.

"Oh, it's beautiful!" Lara spun around, laughing in sheer pleasure. The ship had landed on a sandy spit, crystalline blue water on their right and a rainbow forest on their left. A faint breeze fluttered the leaves, creating a kaleidoscope of colors.

With a nod from Tenn, Lara joined him in removing their helmets. As she ran toward the trees, Tenn's longer stride caught up. "Easy does it, Ensign," he reminded her. "Curb your enthusiasm. Save it for me."

She turned and stared at him. No, despite that sexy smile, he was just fooling around again. He couldn't be serious…could he?

"This spot is splendid, Captain…and there's no way I can go off half-cocked," she teased. "Don't deny you're as excited as I am to find our mission is a success. After all this time…"

"Roger that, but let's reel in our eagerness. Save the euphoria until we finish exploring. You never know what we'll run into."

"Okay, Spoilsport." Grinning, she tucked spacesuit-covered arm around Tenn's, surprised at how comfortable she felt. Her face tingled where the fresh alien air touched her skin. The sensation was invigorating, but it was the man towering over her who offered protection along with excitement.

She could cope—she'd been well trained. But in this gorgeous spot, her annoyance about being treated differently floated away. Rather than bristle at his orders, she felt a tiny thrill at his concern.

They walked over to the colorful trees, their branches spread above them. Lara put out her hand but stopped short of touching. "The bark is quite different from Earth trees," she said, a slight hesitation in her voice. She moved closer. "It's not cracked and peeling. Rather like a chocolate bar—rich brown and smooth. Is it safe to take off my glove and feel it?"

Tenn checked the nanochip computer behind his ear. "No bad vibes. Go ahead."

Laying down her helmet, she removed a glove and skimmed her fingertips over the bark. "It does feel like a candy bar. But even more—" she swallowed as her pupils widened "—like human skin. A baby's soft skin."

Tenn pulled off a glove and laid his large hand flat on the bark. "I'll be damned. It feels quite pleasant. Warm and—"

"Sensuous," added Lara. They glanced at each other, and she giggled. "That's what exploring new planets promised—sensational experiences."

"In both senses of the word," Tenn agreed, chuckling. "Wait till Gordon gets his sticky scientific fingers on this life form. Chocolate candy, indeed."

The two wandered among the trees, inhaling a sense of the place. "The air smells so fresh, so clean," Lara murmured. "I feel happy just breathing it."

"Know what you mean. It's exhilarating." Tenn

turned toward the shore. "I'd like to strip and take a swim in that blue water, but we'd better not try it until Gordon completes all the tests."

Lara squelched a gasp. His choice of the word 'strip' brought on a great visual. She glanced up at Tenn and for once didn't feel like turning his words into a joke. Quibbling would spoil the picture of all those rippling muscles bared to her gaze. He looked back at her as if reading her mind, but she turned away, hiding her smile.

The two strolled along the beach and through the forest, recording their impressions as their five senses absorbed the atmosphere. Tenn concentrated on reporting his observations, and Lara made sure not to distract him.

Gordon could still see them, as no ground cover existed between the trees. No small plants appeared with blossoms to match the glorious colors of the leaves. Although they stopped to peer in all directions, there was no sign of living creatures, no sound of birds chirping or insects buzzing.

"Odd," Tenn muttered. "On such a benign planet, why aren't there more life forms?"

Puzzled, Lara agreed. Yet the air itself hummed a song of delight, putting apprehensions to rest. *It's almost hypnotic, except that I feel so alert, so alive. Whatever is causing that almost inaudible sound, it doesn't impair human senses...* "Gordon's missing all this."

"He'll pop out to eat with us before it gets dark," Tenn replied, "then get back to his computers. If I know Gordon, he'll save his outdoor explorations for tomorrow. His big delight is in the data his computers are pouring out."

They smiled at each other, understanding. In the months the three spent together, there wasn't much they hadn't shared. Only her very private feelings were kept hidden.

"I've an idea. Why don't we stay out for the sun's setting? Watch the planet's two moons rising," she added. "It won't be too dark to see. There's no real night here—just day, twilight, and dusk."

"The wind will pick up as it cools," he warned.

"Shouldn't bother us."

"No, we'll keep warm." Tenn's voice had grown deeper, huskier. As they smiled this time, inside her spacesuit Lara felt a delicious shiver slide down her body. There was something very attractive, very compelling about Tenn. His smile alone could be lethal. But then, all Navy SEALs had that aura of strength and sexuality. She'd better not read too much into that smile. It wasn't exclusive.

Lara hadn't realized how much it affected her until she'd hit solid ground. Aboard, she chucked all such sensations into a mental folder labeled *Daydreams*.

It was as if her training precluded awareness within the confined quarters of the ship. Even with good ventilation, an odor lingered when one got too close. It wasn't unpleasant, just somehow off-putting. She'd swear the scientists had added a neuro-chemical to the ventilating system to help the crew keep their distance. Not being disturbed by sensual urges made for a more efficient mission. Maybe that was why…

Stop imagining, she told herself as pent-up longings seeped through. *It's just this tantalizing air.* "Maybe his flirting isn't just fooling," Lara murmured, too low for Tenn to pick up. "I'll let nature take its course."

Tenn did hear her words, however. Picking up the slightest sound was part of SEAL training. His suggestive glance clued her in, and she felt the heat rush to her cheeks. It was clear he also felt these currents flowing between them. His amused grin contrasted sharply with his blond waves and far-from-innocent baby blues. She tamped down her reaction before her blush gave her away.

A short time later, the sun began to sink behind the forest and the ridge of jagged cliffs beyond. The flaming sunset took her breath away—it was glorious. The lake's surface turned to dazzling glass, reflecting the many shades of red in the twittering leaves. Lara dipped her hand in the water, stirring the images. Pink and purple rippled in tiny waves, blending with a fiery orange. Hot colors, indeed.

Chapter Three

As the sunset faded, the first moon rose to cast a silvery light on the landscape, bathing the two people on shore in luminescence.

Gordon stared as he left the ship to join Lara and Tenn for a beach picnic. His colleagues glittered and shimmered, their images wavering like a mirage. He'd have to touch them to make sure they were really there.

Hurrying over, he reached for them, and then glanced down at his arm. Not only were his colleagues real, but he was glowing, too. A trick of the light. *Neat.* He was too much the scientist to allow the word "magical" to enter his mind. This planet was a find.

With Gordon's reassurance, they leaned against a sand dune and ate from their Instapaks of manufactured taste-alikes—spaghetti in meat sauce, green beans with almonds, and chocolate lava cake. The surroundings so enchanted them, they barely noted the artificial flavors.

"You know, we're lucky to be able to see the second moon," Gordon told his shipmates. "We're here at the right time. It isn't really a moon, I've discovered. It's a comet with an elliptical orbit that passes close to this planet once every six months. It stays overhead for two nights, then returns to deeper space. We've been trying to test its effects on the atmosphere without success, not even with our finely calibrated instruments. But now we're right on the spot. Should get hard data this time."

"Has anyone named the planet?" Lara asked.

"Yes, it's on the space charts as Nacre, chosen for the pearl essence inside an oyster shell. No one has landed here before us. Good thing its glow was seen and recorded by drone ships passing by. These mini-planets are easy to miss."

The three talked idly for a while, enjoying the stillness and beauty of their surroundings. They speculated on what Earth would be like after their return from their year's stint. When the real moon began its disappearing act beyond the planet's curvature, Gordon rose to return to his instruments.

"The comet will show up on the western horizon soon," he called back as he walked away. It'll cross over the lake and then the trees. Be sure to keep your recording devices on. I'll pick up your reactions inside the ship and transfer them to Earth."

"We won't forget," Lara assured him. "And give Akemi our regards when you contact Earth."

His head snapped around. "You're teasing me, right?" He watched her eyelids flutter down. Muttering about different cultures, he shook his head and continued on.

****

The night grew colder. Tenn and Lara walked over to the woods and took shelter under the trees. Despite their elation, it had been a long hard day, and the fizzy air made them sleepy. Each chose a tree to lean on. Minutes passed. Through sleepy, half-closed eyes, Lara became aware of the sky growing lighter. A bright light rose above the horizon, spreading its radiance as it drew closer, agitating the atmosphere. On the ground, everything glistened. A warm breeze stirred the leaves of her tree.

As her body sensed the changes, Lara became fully awake. The air prickled as she breathed, like champagne tickling her nose. She blinked as its effervescence touched her eyelids, lingering on her lashes like fine raindrops.

The tree she leaned against stirred. Shaking her head to clear a momentary dizziness, Lara rose to her feet. Something was happening to the tree. It was so beautiful, glowing in the luminescence. She reached out gently to touch the chocolate bark. It undulated beneath her fingers, a tiny caress.

Suddenly, Lara was overwhelmed with a desire to hug the tree, to tell it she loved it. This wasn't normal. Once again, she shook her head. Strange sentiments filled her, feelings of affection, deep caring. She tried to hold back, but the urge grew irresistible. She threw her arms around the tree and hugged it. Matching her contours, it pressed gently back.

As Lara leaned in and placed her lips on its soft, flesh-like surface, two limbs bent down and stroked her back. She felt warm and safe. Limbs were another word for arms after all, and these felt almost human, even to the twig-like branches at the ends that touched her like fingers.

She had no idea how long she stayed in their embrace, absorbing feelings of acceptance and love. The chocolate fingers caressed her as they turned her around and pulled apart the Velcro closures on her spacesuit. They slid inside to smooth over her breasts and tweak her nipples. She gasped as a rippling thrill raced through her body. Oh, this was weird, but so good…

The feeling of love for the tree, of it becoming a part of her and she of it, grew stronger as the soft chocolate limbs opened her trousers and slid them down. Her head fell back, leaning on the strange arms as they pleasured her, the fingers inside her, twisting and caressing, one fingerlike twig flicking her clitoris until she moaned with arousal.

The tingling air touched every inch of her body, fondling her, while leaves gently brushed back and forth, tickling her face and chest, driving her nipples to sensitive points. Her breath quickened. From her twitching toes to her charged hair clinging to the bark, the thrills flowed, rising…rising…

For a wild moment, she was consumed with rapture. Her orgasm burst forth in a shower of rainbows flaring against the back of her eyelids, sensations more intense than any she had ever known. *Incredible.* The tree absorbed her moisture as the limbs gently moved away, hugging her in return as they slipped back into place.

Dazed and smiling, Lara slid down to the base of the tree and fell into a deep, healing sleep. Red and pink leaves drifted down to cover her and keep her warm.

In the stillness that followed, the trees seemed to nod, communicating in their own leafy language. Underground, the soil stirred.

****

The comet was still heating and agitating the air when Tenn awoke beneath his tree. He felt woozy, turned, reached out, and grabbed hold. Two arm-like limbs were at just the right height to rest on his shoulders, and it was comforting. He wasn't awake enough to question why. His lips touched the chocolate bark and he laughed; it felt like a kiss.

"This isn't Navy protocol," he scolded, fully alert now. He began to back off, to recover his command of the mission. But as he stood there fighting the alien urges, a flood of awareness, of kinship, washed over him. He was joined to the tree in a bizarre fashion, and yet it felt right—strongly, absolutely right. This might be a forbidden experience, but he didn't want to miss it. He'd learned to trust his hunches and thirsted to know more.

His hands, bracing his body against the tree, slid around to hug it. Somewhere, deep inside, Tenn grinned as he remembered old Earth stories about tree huggers. This was the real thing.

The tree beckoned and all thoughts of Earth were blocked. It absorbed his consciousness, creating a link between them. Although he still struggled to understand what was going on, for his training would allow no less, he became pleasurably aware of the two arm-like limbs undressing him. Leaves scratched at his nipples, and warm melting chocolate twig-fingers slid down his body. They took hold of his package, caressing his balls, and began stroking and squeezing his cock. He shuddered.

For a moment, Tenn tried once again to fight this alien sensation, his penis shriveling despite the intimate touch. He was the leader, knew his duty, had to remain in command. But the feeling of loving care was so intense, it soon overwhelmed his automatic reaction. He never dreamed he'd be a party to that old joke with the punch line, "when rape is inevitable, relax and enjoy it." But this, of course, was nothing like that—it was seduction. Exquisite seduction. And here he was, a SEAL on the other side of that equation. Talk about new experiences—*hoo-yah!*

Accepting the inevitable, he relaxed and allowed himself to enjoy every touch. After all, his feelings were being recorded, and scientists on Earth would learn about this fabulous planet and its adoring trees. By letting himself be a guinea pig, he was serving his country. The irony was delicious.

This is one for the history books, was his last rational thought.

His pleasure increased as Tenn gave himself wholly to the experience. His cock was stroked with loving care; the speed and pressure matched his mounting desire. The caring twigs moved higher, trailing along the crack. With a shiver, he squeezed his cheeks together as what felt like a candy "kiss" slid into his asshole. His sexual tension built and built until he could no longer delay the rapture. Breathing rapidly, his cock gripped hard and his asshole fingered, he came, spurting forth with a shout of joy that echoed through the forest.

And then Nirvana…bliss. His semen spread across the tree trunk and was instantly absorbed.

Sliding down in the afterglow, Tenn fell into a sound sleep beneath the tree. Orange and purple leaves fluttered down to cover him as he drifted off, stirring the hairs on his chest with a soothing abrasion.

The night wore on. The comet moved across the sky.

****

Hours later, Lara awoke. She felt marvelous. Giddy. Alive and aware in a new way. The experience surpassed even her fantasies about Tenn. Brushing off the leaves, she climbed back into her clothing. For a sublime moment, she envisioned the tree bending, twisting, and dissolving into warm, pliant flesh until it assumed Tenn's form and face. *Wow!* A shape-shifting lover. With dreams like that, who needed reality?

As she Velcroed the last flap, she saw the man of her dreams walking toward her. He looked abashed, an unusual sight on a SEAL. No, he was more than abashed—he seemed angry. All she'd done was smile at him. A bit warmly, perhaps, but she was still recovering from the night's experience. Was that what made him irritable? More likely, the cause could be found in last night's exposure.

Had Tenn undergone a similar relationship with the trees? How had he reacted to those questing fingers? Did he resist? Was it absolutely necessary for the captain to remain in control?

Well, she wouldn't let him take his anger out on her. His grimace spoiled her mood, and she grew cross. If he had resisted, he was probably disappointed—in himself, for not having the courage to go beyond his male prejudices and accept a new and alien experience. And if he'd succumbed—well, he probably couldn't bear his lapse from customary SEAL behavior. It was a lot to swallow.

Either way, he was mad at himself, and it was her duty to point that out. She wouldn't back down. First, though, she'd have to find out what he'd undergone— or missed out on.

Lara stepped a bit closer. "Tenn?" she said hesitantly.

The Captain glowered.

"Hey, don't take your bad mood out on me." So much for restraint. Hands on hips, Lara raised her chin. "I don't know what you went through last night, but for me the experience was profound. Ecstatic. And if you didn't share a similar earth-shaking episode, I feel sorry for you."

Tenn stared directly in her eyes for several seconds. Then, without warning, he grabbed her, his big arms encompassing even her spacesuit as his lips crushed hers in a burning kiss.

Before she could protest, Lara felt her body responding. *Oh my goodness.* This planet was becoming the stage for all her fantasies. Forgetting her pique, she threw her arms around him, barely reaching around the sides of his space suit to grip his back. As the kiss softened and deepened, she gave herself wholly to it. His tongue slid inside her mouth and her insides tingled, matching the effervescent air surrounding them.

She was breathless when they finally broke apart. Somehow, Lara knew. "You were 'introduced' to the trees, too?" He looked at her—into her. The answer was in his eyes.

"Intimately?" she asked.

He nodded.

"And were you the act-or or the act-ee?" A giggle escaped as she said the words.

Rather than answer, he grabbed her again. Her lips parted under his onslaught, and their tongues began the mating dance. Lara grew so hot she couldn't bear her spacesuit. She helped Tenn as he pulled apart the jacket's Velcro tabs, then she leaned in to undo his tabs as well.

Tenn sat Lara down, kneeled, and pulled off her

boots. He yanked open the lower part of her suit and chucked it along with her underpants. Swiftly, he raised her shirt and bared her torso. Her breasts, flushed pink with excitement, thrust toward him, and he took a deep breath.

Without bothering to do more than open his own suit, Tenn lifted her legs onto his shoulders. Gazing at the glistening pink glory he had exposed, he bent his head and lapped. With one long sweep of his tongue, he set up a tingle that ran from her rear straight up to her coppery pubic hairs. She gasped. Was this real, or was she dreaming?

His gaze returned to her face as his big hands pushed away the sides of her jacket and filled his palms with her breasts. Breathing deeply, he nuzzled between the soft, curving mounds.

"You carry the scent of springtime." He sniffed again, butting his nose back and forth against her nipples. "Lilies of the Valley. So sweet. I've been wanting to do this for the last eight months." His words ground out, as if forced. Gazing at her satiny skin with its rosebud tits, he walked his fingers up from her quivering navel to circle her breasts once more. His thumbnail flicked across her nipples, shooting darts of desire through her. "I pictured them filling my hands, my mouth, as I breathed in your taste. Cinnamon sugar. Dash of nutmeg." He licked his lips. "But in the ship, my hands were tied." With a sly grin he added, "So were my mouth…and my cock."

His deep voice with its sexy, husky tone, even the very words he chose, had her panting. "Don't wait now." She gasped. "I'm more than ready."

He laughed as he picked her up and moved them

farther into the trees. "My fantasy, bawdy astronaut. The reality is better than the dream." Hastily, they finished undressing.

Unable to speak through her wildly beating heart, Lara slid her hand down to caress his cock. With a rough groan, he laid her down and fell on top of her. Their weird and wonderful tree-love following months of abstinence in space acted as a powerful aphrodisiac. Foreplay had been thoroughly taken care of—for now. Tenn needed to be deep inside her.

With a wild desperation, he plunged. Wet and eager, Lara lifted her legs around his waist. They moved together at an exquisitely intense pace, knowing each other's rhythm by instinct. This first time was too quick, and yet it was perfect. Lara's scream of release matched Tenn's shout as he exploded inside her.

Only moments had passed before Lara felt a nudge at her crack as she lay on her side spooned around him. With a delicious sigh, she rubbed her ass against him, feeling his hardness grow. He dropped little kisses all along her spine as he reached around and tickled her clitoris. Her body hummed under his touch.

This time their loving was lazy. Doggy-style fucking was new to Lara. Her body unfolded like a flower as she screamed in delight, still fizzing when Tenn turned her over. He entered her once more, gliding into her slippery channel as far and deep as possible, then sliding in and out as wave after wave of orgasm overtook her. At the last moment, he reached down and finger-tipped her clit. With that tiny movement, they both went off like rockets.

"I think we just launched *Frontier 2*," Lara murmured as they lay sated and content, letting the rising wind fan the leaves that brushed their bodies and cooled them. After a bit, she raised her head and leaned on an elbow, smiling down at Tenn's contented face. "How did it feel to take the passive role last night?" she asked, her fingers tickling his stomach.

He squirmed. "Strange. I don't know how the shrinks will regard my reactions, especially coming from space." He hesitated, then added, "I don't really know how I feel."

"It wasn't so bad, was it?" She teased him. "Sexual pleasure has many facets. I don't mind experiencing them all, as long as they're carried out with love."

"Agreed," Tenn said, rising and pulling her up beside him. "Pleasure is the goal. I know some people enjoy pain, but I'll leave that for the bad guys. There's enough of them around for me to vent my aggressions."

"Yes. You SEALs have mapped the necessary force with amazing skill. You always know the time and place." Lara caught his jaded look. "Heard it too many times, have you? I'm not joking—the whole world admires you. And I'm a fan, too. With my older brother a SEAL, and my younger one a Jarhead, we all live on the edge. Dad's retired Navy and Mom lives inside her computer. She follows all the news, and even forgets to cook when something big is stirring. It's no wonder I ended up in space. The family nicknamed me 'Starchild.'"

"You're no child, Laralove. That's my pet name for you."

"Much more to my liking." Dropping a quick kiss on his cheek, Lara started to dress. "I guess we'd better get back to where Gordon can see us. Don't want him sending out a robo-probe."

Relaxed now, Tenn closed his spacesuit. "About last night…" He smiled warmly at her. Their eyes conveyed shared knowledge. They knew everything that had happened, had joined in the same wild experience. No need for words, and how sweet it was!

Hand in hand, they ran down to the water and splashed their faces. In the delicious air, the private, sensual feelings for Tenn that Lara kept hidden for eight long months leaked out. They had shared more than physical delights. For a few exciting, unforgettable moments, their minds had melded. Now she eyed the buff Navy SEAL with a gleam in her eyes, allowing the full range of her emotions to show.

He was ogling her, too, letting his glances rise and fall with an anticipation that she knew had been buried deep during their journey. Had the tree enhanced not only his lust but Tenn's deeper feelings toward her as well? She toyed with the thought. What was he still holding back?

This planet, Nacre, certainly had a liberating effect on humans. Were other surprises in store for the crew before they left in three days' time?

Turning off her unsettling thoughts, Lara let the cool blue waters pull at her. On impulse, she stripped and ran splashing into the lake.

Startled, Tenn turned around. "Come on in," she called. He stood on shore, eyes watchful, guarding her. "It's okay. The water's fine."

As his nanocomputer assessed the situation, Lara waited, eager to have him beside her, but pleased to be the object of his protectiveness. Her appreciative gaze didn't leave Tenn's body while he stripped and joined her.

"Stars in Space," she whispered as she watched the gorgeous hunk of male dash into the lake. Just staring at that perfect masculine shape did things to her insides. A tough Greek god, lean, muscular, and especially, warm. Then she forgot everything as Tenn dived underneath the water and came up between her legs. Gasping, conscious of the excitement growing inside as he rubbed against her, she began to splash him.

"Sneaky, Captain," she cried, hitting the water hard with the heel of her palm, speeding up her splashing assault. "Are you trying to prove you're truly a seal?"

"How'd you guess?" He laughed, diving under once more and lifting her onto his shoulders. She bent down and ran her fingers through his wet hair, scratching at his scalp.

"Mmm." Tenn leaned his head into her hands. "I like that."

She wriggled against him, laughing as a new thrill arose. He smelled so good, so wet and fresh and male. His hands began to stroke her legs, rubbing the fine hairs so they tickled. Lara sighed. What she felt, she decided as the cool air caressed her back, was pure enchantment.

Chapter Four

Gordon came out of the spaceship to see his crewmates frolicking in the water. "Hey, guys," he called, bouncing with exuberance. He beckoned them closer. "I learned all about the mysterious trace element in the air. Its chemical composition is the same as human pheromones. Maybe that's why the air here is so stimulating! The tests showed that when the comet passes by, its magnetic flares increase their potency."

Tenn and Lara glanced at each other. Well, she thought, at least there was a scientific explanation for their strange night. Not all of it, though. Until further research explained more, she'd credit some of it to magic…

She lifted her eyebrows in question. As if reading her thoughts again, Tenn nodded. "Yes, he needs to know. You tell him, Lara. He'll think I'm putting him on. It'll sound more believable coming from you."

Gordon frowned. "What's up?"

Lara pushed through the water to the shore's edge and rose to her waist. She reached out to Gordon who had hunkered down on the sand. Her fingers touched his knee, and his startled gaze lifted from her bared breasts to her face. Stifling her grin, she grew earnest. "I'm sure our feelings and sensations are being recorded for analysis back on Earth," she said, "and that's good. But while we're here, you've got to experience this planet for yourself—with all your five senses. Come out of the ship when the sun and moon are down, and only the comet's light is bathing the atmosphere. You've got a treat in store."

"What kind of treat?" Gordon frowned. "Tell me more."

The two shook their heads. "I agree with Lara," Tenn said. "This is something you've got to experience for yourself. Trust me."

"Hey, you can't do this to a scientist! I have to know what's going on. I may have to set up a new experiment."

"Take it from me, Pal, this is something you've got to try first," Tenn insisted. "For once in your life, feel before thinking."

"I don't know…" Gordon pouted, but he couldn't remain angry. Something in the air of this planet didn't allow it. Strange, but at the same time wonderful. While Lara and Tenn dressed, he turned and gazed at the rainbow leaves glinting in the sun.

The three spent the day exploring, taking notes and samples. At sunset, Gordon hightailed it back to the ship and his computer, promising to return as suggested. Now the lake beckoned. Answering its call, Tenn and Lara returned, stripped, and swam in the moonlight, the water like velvet stroking their bare skin. The breeze caused tiny wavelets to lap at rarely exposed parts of their bodies, raising goose bumps to tickle and thrill.

Soon the temperature dropped. Prickles turned to shivers. As the air became more agitated, they sensed the comet's arrival. They left the water, and the cooling breeze dried their bodies.

Perfectly comfortable in his nakedness, Tenn rapped on the spaceship's door, signaling Gordon to come out. "Pick a tree," he said, "and wait under it. Lara and I will be over there at the forest's edge." He pointed and moved farther away, leaving a bemused Gordon, still in his spacesuit but minus the helmet, staring at them.

"You two look like Adam and Eve before the fall," he called out as he made his way to a tree.

"Not to worry," Tenn called back. "No snakes here, and the trees bear no fruit."

"I wonder if they ever do," Lara mused. "There's got to be a way they reproduce."

"The scientists will have a field day trying to discover how," Tenn replied. "I'll bet Gordon is already obsessed with finding out."

"You're probably right, but I'm betting the tree will soon take all his attention." Lara chuckled. "It'll give him something else to think about."

Moving farther away, Lara and Tenn gazed at each other. Their breaths came fast in the tingling air. The heightened affection Lara had felt last night returned in a rush, all of it directed at Tenn.

She'd been aware her feelings toward him were growing beyond infatuation. Now they flooded in. He was so good looking—six feet two of surfer-blond, azure-eyed, hard-honed handsomeness. Strong, quick, intelligent, and with a ready laugh during all the calm moments of their flight. When trouble zoomed, he was alert in a flash, never hesitated to make the tough decisions. Lara stood in awe of that ability, her mind always too full of alternate possibilities. She could never assess a situation and instantly know the best way to handle it.

What a demonstration she had when they unexpectedly flew into a Gossamer dust belt beyond the newly discovered outer ring of Jupiter. The microscopic particles, visible only to the computer, acted like bullets. But Tenn's response had been instantaneous. With Gordon barking directions from the computer as she manned the anti-magnetic guns, Tenn maneuvered their ship swiftly through the danger. They zipped through space holes, caught up in a live video game!

When they reached the Kuiper Belt, he'd done it again, skimming around Pluto and diving below the larger particles, shooting them into outer space.

In nanoseconds they were through the belt, leaving her so overdosed with adrenaline she had stared at Tenn's profile, craving a good fuck with her hero to bring her down from the high. She wanted to jump him, swing her legs up, and smother him with kisses as he pounded into her. So intense were her feelings she felt sure they had melted their space suits and penetrated Tenn's cool professionalism, but as far as she could tell, he never stepped out of his captain's role.

"Whew," he had said, his smile impersonal, "that was close. Good work!" Then he'd gripped her shoulder, just as he had Gordon's, leaving her horny but happy with the compliment. She'd been accepted, at last, as an equal member of the crew.

Yes, she and Gordon were lucky to have this commander for their first venture into outer space. Tenn's teasing sense of humor matched hers to a T. In the confines of the ship, he filled the dull periods with wry comments, alternating quips with droll descriptions of training mishaps. When action was required, his orders were crisp and sure, brooking no hesitation. Yet he made everything easy to follow.

As she sat with Tenn under the trees, Lara was filled with a sense of destiny. She and this man were made for each other. They had to be. When she was close to him, it felt so right.

One minute she was sure, but in the next minute the comet passed by. Was she rushing things? Could he possibly feel the same? There was so much she still didn't know about him, even after eight months. On the deeply personal side, she knew very little. A smidgen of doubt sneaked into her feeling of rightness and tore a small hole.

****

Tenn studied Lara's face, read her thoughts, her hesitation. He understood and absorbed her emotions, his own rapidly morphing into passion. Although he'd never allowed it to show, especially after their escape from the Kuiper Belt when her ardent glances had pushed him to the edge of his professionalism, Tenn had given her his heart almost as soon as they met. The part he could spare, that is.

They were in the field's briefing room before takeoff when he became aware of her presence and its effect on him. He'd done the routine flight checks for hunting new planets often enough to split his concentration. Half of it took in Lara, nicely rounded coppery redhead with a smile as bright as the antique pennies he'd polished for his collection. Her short hair curled at the ends and rested on the soft skin of her cheeks. Darker eyelashes pointed to perfectly shaped lips, a turned up nose, and warm brown eyes like molten fudge. She was slender, but her toned body couldn't be hidden, even in a spacesuit.

Her alert attention and quick responses to the admiral's questions endeared her to him from the start. She was a teammate worth acquiring for their long flight. Yet when he read the statistics in her file before they met, and noticed how fragile she looked in the attached photo, he knew she'd be a problem.

He would want to protect her, and this could interfere with the mission. Space was too dangerous. His opposing feelings warred within him, making him fight to keep her out. Weren't there enough people in his life needing his protection? He sighed. If he was ordered to go along with it, he'd override his feelings, keep his damn doubts to himself.

It was second nature to hide his reactions, and he would do so for the entire mission. But they would get to know each other—intimately, he decided back then. Even though it had to be postponed, that was a given.

As Lara leaned back farther on the tree trunk, the tantalizing aroma of chocolate wafted through the air. "When I first heard your name, I thought Tenn was short for Tennessee," she said, "But you don't sound like a Southerner."

"Strictly Western—I grew up in Arizona. My mom was a Lit major and fell into English poetry. That's how I got to be Tennyson. My brother's name is Dylan, middle name Thomas. No relation to that long ago folk singer—just another of Mom's favorites."

"Are you into poetry, too?" she asked.

"You mean, beyond 'Men don't make passes at girls who wear glasses?'" He grinned and shrugged. "Hated it when I was a kid, but in college I ran across some old-time war poems. Pretty solid stuff." He looked as if he would say more but clammed up instead.

Holy Quasars, Lara thought. *I've embarrassed him. Hotshot SEAL with a sensitive side, though it would take him a light-year to admit it. I could fall in love with this guy…if I haven't already.*

"That should give us something new to talk about on the long journey home," she said, her lips curving upward at the corners. At Tenn's disgusted look, Lara chuckled. We could add some limericks…you know, Roger the Lodger…"

"That's more like it."

She lifted her chin. "One mystery solved, but you have another—that little white scar on your neck. Was it from a Vampire bite?" She fought to keep a straight face as his right eyebrow arched.

"You can find out by licking it," Tenn told her, all innocence. "I'm sure your tongue will be able to tell if it was made by teeth marks."

She blushed as he added, "Gotcha!"

Tenn reached out, tugging her close until Lara's head rested on his shoulder. As the two sat companionably under the tree, a limb stretched out and curved across their backs. It poked at them, goading them on. They glanced at the chocolate fingers, then at each other. Lara started to giggle, but Tenn just smiled as he leaned forward. "I guess the trees don't need us anymore."

"Yet they want us to get closer," Lara said dreamily. "They're so full of love, they want us to share it."

"I'm not sure I buy that explanation; you're making them awfully human," he responded. "But then again, I can't account for last night, either. So let's try your theory."

With a finger under her chin, Tenn raised her head and pressed his lips to hers, sliding them back and forth, licking until hers parted. As her breathing intensified, his tongue slid inside her eager mouth. Her body aligned with his, and the passion of the night before ignited between them.

Already naked from the swim, unwilling to break the kiss, they slid their hands over air-tingled skin as they lowered themselves to the soft ground. The tiny vibrations the kiss had started turned into trembling thrills as they reached out and touched. As she mindlessly caressed him, lost in the rhythm of his hard muscles rippling beneath her fingers, he suckled her breasts, bit lightly as he moved down her body, turned her around, and licked every spot his teeth had touched of her magically responsive flesh.

"What's this?" Tenn asked, his hand sliding down her back to rest at the base of her spine. He ran his fingers through a fuzzy patch of baby hair, just above the crack in her ass.

Half turning around, she hid her face in his chest. "When I was little, my daddy told me it was the vestiges of my tail," she mumbled. "Does it bother you?"

"Laralove, you've just shown me a brand new erogenous zone." He kissed the spot, his lips pulling at the fine hairs, then ran his tongue down the crack till he lapped at her clit.

"Holy Pulsars," Lara whispered. "I expected you to be a magnificent lover, but the way you make me feel is out of this world."

Tenn chuckled. "And so it should be. Did you count on this rapture, Ensign? Is it the SEALs' reputation, or my own powerful personality?"

"Mmmhmm…"

Still grinning, Tenn moved back up, rolled her over with just a touch of his finger, and rubbed against her. He tickled her under the arm, then kissed the spot as she quivered. His lips closed around a nipple, running his teeth along it, then paid the same compliment to the other. As she moaned in pleasure, he slid down, nibbling on her stomach before stroking her with his cock, warming every part of her inside and out. Her hands scrambled to touch every part of him, fingers combing through his pubic hairs, nails scratching lightly. What fun to discover they had so many erogenous zones in common. Her long fingernails became entangled in curly blond hairs. She loved the way he groaned as she snagged them. And he smelled like hot sex, his scent alone drugged her. Sliding up to lick him under his arm, she puckered her lips to pull on the hairs there as well. Tickling followed and he squirmed, distracted her with another deep tonguing kiss, then sucked her lower lip into his mouth.

Their foreplay could have gone on forever. Yesterday's experience had intensified their sensations. But on this night, there was no stopping short. As the comet swept across the sky, the very air stirred their emotions to a fever pitch. All night long, they wallowed in mind-blowing orgasms in every position their heated imaginations could conjure up.

"Loving you is incredible." Lara purred a little later as Tenn began this time by sucking her toes. He drew each one into his mouth, then nipped at the nail. His tongue slid between each toe while new thrills ran up her legs and into her core. She gasped at the exquisite eroticism, bit the back of his heel, then licked her way up his body in teasing return. Climbing on top, she rode him, leaning forward so that a breast fell into his eager open mouth. Their rhythm was perfect, their orgasm perfection.

Toward dawn, they fell asleep in each other's arms, bodies meshing in wondrous harmony. Softly drifting leaves covered them while they were watched over by the caring, benevolent trees.

****

Gordon, meanwhile, had parked himself under a tree, reached out, touched it, tasted it—and fell in love.

His scientific mind fought the delightful but alien sensations much longer than had either Lara or Tenn. The strangeness was unreal, and nothing could faze a scientist more than inexplicable unreality. Part of his mind analyzed what was occurring even as his eyes took in the arm-like limbs forming on the tree. His fingers ran over the satiny chocolate colored bark. His tongue lapped at its unusual sweetness.

The tingling air surrounded him, lightly tapping his skin, arousing his nerve endings, and tantalizing his senses. *Pheromones,* he kept telling himself as his spacesuit was stripped away, but the sound of his whispered voice soon lost the first syllable as he gave in to the 'mones' of delight.

"Man, I'm in love with a tree," Gordon whispered. "Wait till the guys at Cal Tech hear about this...not that I could ever tell them."

He waited for the flush of embarrassment he knew would flow through him. Instead, the current coursing

34

through his body was one of joy, of sexual arousal that he knew would be satisfied, and of the rare sensation of letting go, of permitting his reason to shut down.

The chocolate twig fingers undressed and stroked him, rubbing against his nipples, sliding down his taut stomach, caressing his balls with gentle pressure, building his response. They slid forward to squeeze and stroke his cock, then backward to slide along his crack and probe. He trembled. The sensation of being penetrated, shocking at first, gave way to thrilling strokes. Sensitive nerve endings resonated within his core. Testicles tightened, relaxed, his cock growing hard. The motions excited, yet the mood was tender, so tender that even through his arousal he felt enveloped by love.

His orgasm came almost too soon, but it was so powerful a blast, Gordon knew he would never forget it. Never forget how his mind disappeared, how he lost himself in the whirlwind of sensations. Who would have expected an alien world to offer such delights?

As the tree absorbed his semen, soft yellow and amber leaves tickled him, hastening his slide to the base of the tree. "How does it work?" he whispered dreamily as his head came to rest in a comfortable fork between the trunk and a large root. "Is it all chemical?"

Before another question loomed, he fell into a deep and peaceful sleep.

Chapter Five

Only one night remained before the comet disappeared behind the planet. Then Nacre would once more revolve around its sun with a single moon…until the next time the strange air began to throb with agitated pheromones spilling through the atmosphere.

That last night, when the comet had already begun to recede from view, the crew enjoyed a final picnic on the beach. All knew they had shared the same bizarre but fantastic experience. Any remaining traces of hostility or jealousy among them had dissolved. Nacre's exotic atmosphere had brought them closer than ever.

As the air grew more luminescent, they wandered over to the forest and sat down under the same trees. Love and loyalty flowed between them. Within all three were the zeal of the scientist, the daring of the explorer, the creativity and nurturing of the female.

They knew in their hearts that once more aboard ship their training would take over. They would function as a caring but impersonal team until they landed back on Earth. But for this night, in a knowing silence, they undressed each other and loved. Loved with hands and mouths, with kissing and thrusting, with touching and fondling, with no opening left unexplored in a passionate sexual marathon.

Gender didn't exist. At special moments, Lara knew that Gordon was imagining Akemi, and for those moments she was Akemi, sharing another's innermost being. For Tenn, she was Lara and Eve as well, the unique essence of all females. She, herself, felt loved by two men, absorbing their strength, their aggression, and their protection.

Lost in a hedonistic fog, she didn't know whose lips she kissed or where, whose cock she sucked so deep, whose penis was inside her, bringing her to bliss. And hands—hands were everywhere, touching, stroking, tickling, scratching, probing. Who was shouting? Who was moaning? Who was gasping? Who was sighing? The sounds became a melody.

Their bodies, sometimes clumsy on Earth in the urgency of desire, here moved with the flowing grace of a symphony, a complex song in three-part harmony. Fantastic, mind-blowing orgasms struck all three simultaneously. Their coda was a climax of such exquisite pleasure, words could never express it. Nor were words necessary. This night existed in another dimension...

A cool breeze caressed them as the three fell asleep locked in each other's arms.

****

When they awoke the next morning, there was no awkwardness. Instead of embarrassment, they laughed in glee. What a night to remember! They ran into the blue water of the sunny lake, washed, then donned their space suits. As they headed back to the ship, Lara turned to bid farewell to the trees.

"Hey, guys, look!" she shouted, pointing. Tenn and Gordon turned and stared. Tenn's eyebrows flew up, Gordon's mouth dropped open. Next to each of the trees they had personally experienced sprouted a little green bush.

Lara's baby tree had unfurled a pink blossom, Tenn's stripling an orange one, and Gordon's sported a tight yellow bud. Even as they watched, it began to unfurl. Farther back, small green shoots could be seen emerging from the soil beside the other trees.

Gordon blinked. "We must have fertilized them…somehow," he said. "The pheromones in the air here are Earthlike. The trees seem to need human sexual excretions to reproduce. What a fantastic symbiosis!"

"Don't jump to conclusions," Tenn warned. "My turn to call a halt. All of this could be coincidence. Before you deliver that paper to your Cal Tech colleagues, let the computer analyze everything. Let it deduce what it can. Research scientists or no, the guys at home are going to find our story impossible to believe."

"They're not the only ones." Gordon heaved a sigh. "I may be dreaming this entire experience. You'd better pinch me, Captain."

As Tenn looked from Gordon to Lara, she too wondered if they were in the midst of a strange communal dream. But no. She turned toward Tenn with a joyous smile, knowing her love couldn't be misinterpreted.

"It's real," he said, turning to pinch Gordon's nose. "Unbelievable but real. A miracle to our minds, but just another stage of evolution. Out here in space, life has evolved differently." He turned back to Lara. "And how good it is! A great leap forward for Mother Nature."

"I hope," she said hesitantly, "that when we colonize Nacre, we don't change anything. It would be a shame to be thrown out of Paradise a second time."

Tenn nodded, looking uncomfortable. Needing no words, she knew they were both remembering the devastation Earthlings had brought to their own planet.

But Gordon, always the ambitious scientist, appeared not to hear, for he challenged Lara. "This may be just the planet we've been searching for," he protested. "We need to colonize it before Earth uses up all its resources. We'll need time to prepare. It's vital that I deliver my report right away."

"This time it's you who's going off half-cocked," Tenn rebuked him. "We mustn't jeopardize what we've found here. I don't want to see big money gobbling up all the resources. We've got to hold the line."

"Yes, Gordon," Lara added. "We can't allow greed to destroy Eden. You've seen what happened to Earth in the past. We're still struggling to survive the drastic consequences. This loving planet may offer man—and woman—our only chance to grow, to become more than we are. Here we might learn to truly care for each other and the world we live in."

"But science has to chart the way," Gordon insisted. "These discoveries will benefit mankind. We may need Nacre sooner than we think…"

Tenn erupted. "You're a fool! Your narrow mind will cause the destruction of all of us."

Gordon's mouth tightened. "Who appointed you God?" His words dropped like stones.

Tenn's stare grew cold. His face hardened. "I'm the Captain, Lieutenant. That's another name for God."

Gordon was primed for a fight, but he had no chance of winning. Not against Navy protocol, even this far from home. And not against the pull of Nacre.

Lara reached out and put an arm around both men. "Let's stop this right now. See, you're agitating the trees."

Where they stood the air was still, but as they turned to the forest, they could see the leaves blowing wildly about. Another phenomenon. "If nothing else, this planet should have taught us there is a better way!" She urged them toward the ship.

The two men continued trying to stare down the other, but inch by inch, their bodies relaxed. The tension eased. Gordon's protests faded away as the loving power of the planet seeped into his mind. "Maybe there is another way," he mumbled. "But what if…"

"I'm sure when they hear our story, there'll be mobs lining up to emigrate." Tenn saw the moment Gordon accepted his point. Grinning, he punched his arm. "Man, this is the wildest fucking find since Viagra!"

The captain turned serious again. "We have to ask ourselves if telling all is the wisest action we can take…for Earth and for Nacre. Once the media get hold of the story, they'll turn the planet into a circus. We've found something very special here. It's our responsibility to see that it isn't destroyed."

Seared by Tenn's penetrating glance, Gordon slowly nodded.

"I think," Lara cut in, "that the experiment should be verified before the news is made public. More testing needs to be done. We haven't explored other areas of the planet. What do you say we persuade the powers that be of the need to return, maybe next year? At the right time, of course! We can suggest projects worth implementing that would require a larger ship for equipment, and a few technically oriented colleagues to join us."

Tenn agreed. "We'd choose those with compatible personalities, of course."

"Yes!" said Gordon excitedly. "More scientists. We need to explore the rest of the planet and test our observations. Make sure it's truly safe before colonization is planned."

The three looked at each other. Smiles broke out.

"We owe it to our trees to be very careful," Lara said. "They're family now."

Tenn blew out a puff of air he hadn't realized he'd been holding. He was indebted to the trees for the most space-shattering sex of his life. But it was more than that. When Gordon first talked of plans to deliver a paper, he'd been uneasy. He couldn't put it in words, but he was human, as well as a SEAL. Lara's idea of family was fanciful, of course, but in his gut, he knew that in some way beyond his comprehension, it was true.

For just a second, the crew reached out and touched gloved hands. They gazed at the forest, letting the tingling air caress their faces one last time. Then they pulled down their visors and reverted to official mode.

As they climbed aboard the spaceship, Lara turned around and waved. "We'll be back!" she called to the trees. She could almost hear the refrain of that long ago song, "Love is in the Air."

A wind sprang up, rustling the kaleidoscope leaves. Reds and pinks, yellows and purples whispered back to them. They would be waiting.

Settling into her contoured chair, Lara murmured, "I wonder what we'll find when we return. Will the Earth still be the same?"

Tenn heard her wistful sigh through his headphones. He, too, felt a sense of loss at leaving the shining planet. But it felt good to be heading home. On this journey he'd found more than a planet. He'd found Lara. And in doing so, perhaps…he'd found a part of himself.

Lifting his visor with one hand and hers with the other, Tenn twisted his neck for a last soul-searing kiss until Earth.

At the computer, Gordon heard the sucking sound and applauded. "There's this raven-haired lab tech back at Cal who'd be ideal for conducting research. She specializes in DNA analysis. I told you about Akemi, didn't I? She's most…efficient. I think I can persuade her to try out for field work in space next year."

"Uh, good idea," Tenn said as he lifted his mouth from Lara's and shoved their visors back down. "There certainly are incentives. You said this, uh, Akemi, wears her hair in a long black braid?" He turned and winked at Lara.

Behind his visor, Gordon smiled. "Right down to her sweet spot."

At the console, a green light came on. "Computer's all revved," Gordon said. "Time to take control, Captain."

She watched as Tenn leaned over the ship's controls, his movements confident, his mind, she knew, now completely absorbed by the problems of lift-off.

Checking that the hatches were locked, a newly confident Lara strapped herself in. As she rocked with the blast-off, her spirits lifted.

Blowing a kiss to Nacre still in sight down below, she turned her thoughts to home—and to joyful memories. Her gaze switched to Tenn's broad back, and her thoughts sizzled. If only he knew!

But, hey, he did know. She could sense it.

What came next? Did he share all her feelings? Or only the sexual ones? She could hardly wait to find out. Settling back in her seat, Lara began making plans for a thrilling future. *Hoo-yah!*

Part Two
The Second Expedition

Chapter Six

"You'll love it in space, Akemi. The thrill of seeing a new planet for the first time—it's indescribable." Gordon's eyes gleamed. "And Nacre is a world of wonders. It's a privilege to work there. The perks are…" For a moment, those shining eyes looked inward at a wild, faraway landscape. "…truly out of this world."

Deep red cushions lined the futon where they sat in Akemi's San Diego apartment. The spicy scent of chrysanthemums hung in the air. Licking his lips, Gordon smiled at the picture she made. An oversized pink sweatshirt reached midway to her thighs, swamping her. Beneath the DNA spiral printed across her chest in four colors lay the words, "Genes have more fun."

The petite widow stood up and flung her black braid behind her. He couldn't pull his eyes away as it bounced on her hips. She followed the track of his glance, the corners of her pixie lips tilting upward as if she mentally scratched up a chalk mark. *What the hell.* He couldn't hide his feelings any longer.

"Here we go again, Gordy-san. You know I can't leave Kouji for a year."

Gordon reached for her hand and pulled Akemi down onto his lap. He rested his cheek on her head, breathing deeply of her flowery shampoo blending with her own sweet scent. "Your mother and father adore him. Nothing would please them more. And when he starts pre-school, he'll have new games and new friends to keep him busy."

"But he'll forget who I am in a year!" she wailed. "Kouji's only four."

"No he won't. Space communications have leaped ahead. Remember that video I borrowed from the lab at CT? The one about photon tunneling and wormholes? We'll set up an account with the new laser cam-phone outfit. You'll be able to see and talk to Kouji every day in 3-D. In fact, the hologram is so real, you can reach out and touch." He placed his hands on her shoulders and squeezed, willing Akemi to see the image in his head.

"I wish I could tell you how fantastic this planet is. If it weren't classified, I'd describe marvels you wouldn't believe." His wistful expression lingered. "I can hardly wait to return, but it will be so much better with you there, too. And don't forget, when you get back to Earth, you'll be a pay grade higher."

"I don't know…"

"Opportunities like this don't come often. You'll always regret it if you miss out."

"I won't be the only female, will I?"

"Indeed not. Aerospace engineer Lariana Stone is returning. You know, Lara. She was a crew member on my last mission. And the comet expert from the lab, Jenny Duncan, is being considered to analyze the meteorite samples right where they land. She's so thrilled at the idea, she's singing at her microscope. With your DNA studies, you'll fit right in."

"How many will we be?"

"You and I will be two of the eight scientist-technicians, all compatible couples. That's important for exploring Nacre. You'll soon know why." Tongue in cheek, he tickled her palm. "The other woman, Beyatriz Cardozo, is from Brazil. Bey's an astrophysicist, a pilot, and a skydiver! We'll have a blonde, a redhead, and two brunettes." He smacked his lips, his smile turning sly.

She glared at him, shook her head. "That's shallow."

"C'mon," he wheedled, "it's just man talk."

"Well, what about the men? Have we a wavy, a straight, and a curly? And maybe a kinky, too?"

"I don't know about the guys' hair," his laugh was self-conscious, "but we may run into kinky stuff on Nacre."

Before she could question him further, he hurried on. "There's Stan Lieder, a Swiss M.D., specializing in space medicine. Early on, he attended grad school in the U.S. with Jenny. They've got a thing going, if I'm reading the signs right.

"We've also got an East-European specialist in microbial diversity, Dmitri Petrov, with a sideline in robotics. Quiet guy, you have to dig to get to know him. And my buddy, Tennyson James, will captain the space ship again, with Lara as first mate and me as co-captain. Shortly after they returned from the first mission, Tenn and Lara got engaged." Gordon raised suggestive eyebrows.

Akemi ignored his implication. "Sounds strange to call that odd-looking vehicle a ship. I love sailing, love the water. But this so-called 'ship' will zoom through nothingness." She shuddered.

"Space isn't that empty. Believe me, we're eager to avoid obstacles—that's why, even with computer assistance, so much navigation is required, at least for now. New propulsion systems are not far off in the future. But for this trip you'll be asleep most of the time. As for the rest,"—he ran his tongue over his lips—"I'll be with you. What's more, you'll find that being awake and asleep are both new experiences on Nacre."

"You're being cryptic again."

Gordon grinned, leaned forward, and stole a quick kiss. "Even if I could explain, the planet is so extraordinary, you'd accuse me of making it up. In a few months you'll see it for yourself—all will become clear soon after we land."

Setting her on her feet, Gordon rose. He trailed a finger along her collarbone, inwardly smiling at her quick shiver. "I'm counting on you to join the mission. It won't be the same without you."

"Well..." Standing on tiptoe, Akemi slid her arms around Gordon's neck and ran her silvered nails through his dark hair. "I'll think about it. I don't want to lose you for another year. The last was bad enough."

He pulled her closer. "So you missed me, huh?"

Tilting her head up, she ran the tip of her tongue along the lips he'd just moistened. "Maybe a tiny bit."

"Mmm." Cross-eyed so he could watch, Gordon looked down at that pink tongue. With quickened breath, he squeezed her to him so tightly, the pressure in his jeans became unbearable. Easing her a fraction away, he continued. "Let me show you how much I missed you. We can seal the deal with a spaceman's kiss, guaranteed to put you in orbit!"

Akemi rolled her eyes, but her lips still clung to his.

He placed his long-fingers on each beguiling globe of her ass, pinched lightly, and carried her into the bedroom. Dropping onto her bed, he pulled her on top of him, gathered up her thigh-length sweatshirt, and bunched it around her shoulders. She wore nothing underneath. Taking a small, silky breast in each hand, he fondled her tits.

Shivering at his touch, she fumbled to unbutton his shirt. She rubbed her nipples against his smooth chest, humming with enjoyment, and his heart swelled at the sound.

He moved his hands down to curve around her butt and squeeze the satin globes. "Now, when we make love on Nacre," he said, pressing against her pelvis, "we'll be bouncing from the lighter gravity—not much, but just enough to add an extra zing to our joining." With one hand on her back and the other on her ass he demonstrated, holding her tightly while he bounced rapidly up and down.

Her squeals dissolved into murmurs of "yes, yes, yes…"

She sprawled on the bed while he finished undressing them both. "We have enough time," he assured her. "Just don't scream too loud and wake up Kouji."

"Oh, you." Akemi punched him in the stomach and climbed back on top. "Let's see how long you can hold back your groans."

Chapter Seven

A dreary painting framed in gilt hung on the wall behind the director's chair. Its protective glass reflected the desk light, turning the picture of peasants toiling in a wheat field into a smoky mirror.

Dmitri Petrov stared at his own face in the wavy glass, his eyes avoiding the man at the desk. No emotion showed on his countenance, but inwardly he quaked. His hair felt as if it were lifting off his scalp. The East Europe Federation, with the Kremlin for its headquarters, had summoned him. The unexpectedness left him edgy, especially when he saw his boss at the Institute already in the room.

The heavy door closed behind him with a barely audible clang. Added to the closed-in stuffiness of the windowless room, the air held a lingering odor of fear. He waited, knowing the silence was deliberate. A minute ticked by.

Dmitri felt the sweat pop out on his forehead. He clenched his fists to keep from fidgeting. Another minute passed; he could wait no longer. "Is there something wrong with my appointment to the space mission?" he asked, his hands clasped behind him to hide the tremor.

A pained smile crossed the director's lips. "Your assignment to the space crew of *Frontier 2* has been approved." His dry voice carried ominous overtones.

"You have been called here only as a reminder." He rose from behind his enormous desk, the mirrored landscape revealing a short, squat villain of a man with bushy eyebrows and a drooping mustache. His voice deepened with menace. "Any information helpful to the Federation must be immediately reported."

As Dmitri began to sputter, the head of the Institute cut in quickly. "Petrov knows the protocol." He glared, but Dmitri couldn't hold back his protest.

"Commandant, this is a scientific expedition, run by the International Interplanetary Society." He felt shamed as his voice quavered. "Everything accomplished by the IIS will be published, for all the world to see."

The director's nostrils flared, his breath causing his moustache hairs to flutter. "Nevertheless, you are first and foremost a representative of the EEF. As a citizen, *Doctor* Petrov, you have obligations. Do not allow your scientific enthusiasm to impinge on your duty."

The voice was cold, relentless. Dimitri needed no further warning. The government wanted him to spy. Unable to hide his reaction, he looked away.

"How is Olga Petrovna?" the director asked. "A charming woman, your mother. Is she still living in your dacha, manipulating her little robots? I have long been interested in women with clever minds."

Such subtlety. Always the threat before he was allowed to leave. "My mother is well, thank you. I will give her your regards." He wouldn't forget that. The director waved his hand in dismissal.

Stooping, he passed through the heavy office door, designed for shorter men. Once in the lobby, he reached for the handkerchief in his breast pocket, removed his glasses, and slowly patted the moisture from his face. When his heartbeat returned to normal, he buttoned his overcoat and stepped out of the building. The long coat was sable-lined, but at moments like these, he regretted the price.

A limousine was waiting, his colleague already inside, but Dmitri turned away. Pulling a Persian lamb military style cap from a pocket, he fingered the curly fur, unwinding a tight ringlet in his frustration. Looking down he scowled, wound the black fur around his thumb, and popped it back in place. Then he pulled out the earflaps tucked inside, placed the hat on his head, and stomped off. His long legs headed out of the square toward a time-darkened tavern visible a block away.

He would sit in the bar, breathe in air redolent of wine and vodka and earlier, happier days. One or two drinks and he would hear once again the stories of his grandparents' escapades to become heroes of the revolution. He never did straighten out which revolution his mother and her comrades were talking about, there had been so many, but those were the glory days, starting with the race for space, and Sputnik coming in first! He had listened to the tales many times while growing up, proud of his engineer ancestors involved in the first launch. Yes, he would wash down his memories of the little boy on his grandfather's knee, sitting so still they would forget he was there.

At the far end of the bar, a lone violinist sawed away at a melancholy gypsy tune. Sitting here where it was warm and dark, he would unwind from his fright about being dropped from the mission. Yes, he would see Beyatriz again, kiss those full red lips once more. An ache began to pulse behind his right eyebrow.

Would she still feel the same? Would the heat flare up between them as it had in Rio? It must.

Forcing his shoulders to relax, Dmitri called to the bartender for a bottle of Stoli Elit. Tonight he deserved it.

Chapter Eight

Now that their ship could fly directly to Nacre, the journey with hyperdrive shortened to six months. The fifth member of the expedition, Commodore Stan Lieder, with a string of letters besides his M.D., in charge of health and microbiology, checked the crew one last time. He pronounced all in excellent shape, his smile even broader when he delivered the news to Jenny Duncan, the sweet-natured comet expert.

Tenn and Lara, aware that Stan and Jenny were already old 'friends,' caught that special smile and the answering blush. They grinned at the honey blonde. Was a romance brewing here, too? What would Nacre's effect be on this couple? Lara wondered. Something remarkable, no doubt.

Akemi turned out to be as delightful as Gordon described her. A head shorter than everyone else on the expedition, she was shy to begin with, but soon was teasing Gordon, making him rumble with half-concealed laughter. She had a wicked sense of humor and the subtle interplay of cultures—Chinese, Japanese, and altogether global—heightened the attraction between the two. It hung in the air; Lara could feel it. There'd be hot times on the old planet this year! "Hoo yah."

As his earphones picked up her whispered exclamation, Tenn turned to gaze at Lara. She turned slightly, flicked her eyes at the couple, and he nodded. Chalk one up. Funny how such an old expression lingered. Did anyone still know what chalk was once used for?

Looking around, she focused on Dmitri, noting his blank face. *If only Dmitri doesn't spoil it for us all...* She scowled, not wanting a snake in her Garden of Eden. Something about the East European left her uneasy. She had met him before, but didn't recall the shifty look appearing now and then in his eyes. He seemed different today, and so staid. How would he mix with their highly animated Brazilian astrophysicist, she whose hobby was extreme sports? Well, if anyone could lighten whatever burden the man carried, it would certainly be sunny, vivacious, "call me Bey" Beyatriz.

Petrov met Cardozo at a space propulsion conference in Rio. Tenn and Lara attended, too, and they spotted the moves the pair made. Dmitri, with hair like white gold, and the dark, feisty expert in astrophysics had clicked. The tall, handsome couple stood out in the crowded ballroom, making it easy for Tenn and Lara to keep an eye on them. By the time the final paper had been read, they'd signaled thumbs-up on the last two choices for the mission to Nacre.

What had changed since then? Once on board, Beyatriz, bubbling over with enthusiasm, examined everything in the ship. As she bounced on a bunk mattress, teasing eyes sending messages, her space-suited arms swung about, smacking Dmitri's lower back. He staggered for a moment, listening to her voluble apology with a strained smile. So much more formal than his smiles at the conference, Lara thought, but was there longing in his glance, too? Well, one way or another, the mission was fully staffed. She tuned out her worries.

Experts in microbial diversity, pedology, genetics, electronics, neurology, and even alien psychopathology—Lara's second expertise, everyone on the mission had two or more—occupied comfortable bunks in *Frontier 2*, the enlarged spaceship captained by newly promoted Tennyson James. On shore, he was now a Rear Admiral. Aboard ship, he was still Captain to his crew.

On this voyage, too, the air in the cabin contained neuro-chemicals that discouraged aggression, sexual or otherwise. The ship encountered no gossamer dust belts or other space debris. The days flew by with only minor problems to break the monotony.

When he wasn't involved in running the ship, Gordon gravitated toward Akemi. To fill the long hours, she taught him some Japanese phrases. When his pronunciation of *arigatoo* (thank you), *sumimasen* (pardon me), and *Ofuro wa doko desu ka?* (Where is the bathroom?) came through the crew's earphones, they laughed themselves silly.

"How do you say, 'I love you'?" Gordon asked her. Akemi looked away. "We don't say that in Japanese."

"You don't? But you do fall in love?"

"Of course, silly. Do you doubt me?"

"Well, can you talk dirty and still be polite?"

"I don't like that word, but we have illustrated books that instruct us on bedroom behavior. One is called *Shunga*, images of spring, and it celebrates the pleasures of the flesh. It's sensual and erotic, not at all dirty."

"Sorry, that's a hangover from my early days

growing up in a slum. I'd like to see that book."

"Someday, when I'm sure you'll treat it with reverence. Now you can get by with *Daisuki desu.*"

"And that means?" he coaxed. Watching, Lara caught Akemi redden.

"I like you very much," came the soft reply.

Gordon's smile stretched to reach his helmet. Although the doctored air slowed some of his responses, his desire for Akemi leaked out whenever he gazed at her. Lara and Tenn watched the affair blossom, once again signaling thumbs-up.

Around her neck, Lara wore Tenn's SEAL pin on a platinum chain, the eagle, anchor, pistol, and trident now circled by orbiting stars. The feelings fired up on their first visit to Nacre hadn't diminished once they'd returned to Earth. In fact, their on-and-off courtship, broken by missions pulling them in different directions, only heightened their longing to be in each other's arms. Their short furloughs together grew combustible. They'd barely hugged a hello before clasps were opened, zippers pulled down.

Although Lara accepted Tenn's pin, she didn't coax him for a ring. They still had a lot to learn about each other. Even though the sex was super, a lifetime commitment was too damn serious to take lightly. Nevertheless, the pin resting on her chest warmed her throughout.

When the big day came at last, and they were both chosen to staff and pilot *Frontier 2*, Lara broke into a happy dance. Watching, Tenn pulled her to him, swung her around, and kissed her neck below her swaying hair.

"Uh oh," she whispered as the tingle died down,

"We've forgotten we have an audience."

Tenn looked up, noticed the Brass standing near, conspicuously looking in the other direction. "Okay. I'll take a rain check...but not for long." Sneaking in a pinch to her butt, he'd let her go, once more becoming the consummate SEAL.

Now, as they neared the planet, the crew's anticipation grew to a fever pitch. Before Lara realized it, she was peering down at her beloved trees waving their pink and orange, red and purple leaves as if in welcome. They landed smoothly. No "oof" necessary, this time. Lara giggled, remembering.

****

Passengers and equipment were unloaded on the beach, lab and sleeping pods set up, and communications with home base quickly established. The crew had less than a week before the comet approached, when the effervescent air would turn from tingle to zing. Whenever they met that first week, Tenn, Lara, and Gordon exchanged secret smiles—the new scientists were in for a fabulous surprise.

Work soon settled into routine. With more specialists at specific assignments, Gordon concentrated his studies on the alien soil. The ground around the base had been thoroughly tested. He needed to gather samples from farther afield.

Absorbed in her experiments, Akemi had less time for Gordon than he had hoped. He nagged her, but after a few hot kisses, she would reluctantly push him aside. Only her nightly holographic calls to her son Kouji interrupted her intense absorption in the samples she studied—identifying the genetic components of the chemicals within the brilliant leaves. He grumbled

58

about her persistence, but loved her all the more.

Pans on her desk held a solution preserving the leaves in their riot of colors. They lay within, quivering at each draft of air. As the comet drew closer, the breeze quickened. Soon the rapid movement of the leaves indicated changes in the atmosphere.

Gordon's restlessness grew. The far-off jagged cliffs had been calling to him since his first visit to Nacre. The bleakness of the cliffs backing up to the forest's loveliness created a shocking contrast, and his scientist's brain demanded an explanation. He needed to test soil samples from the other side.

On the day before the comet's arrival, he gave in to his urge to explore. Packing a few instruments, sample containers, a sandwich and a bottle of water, he wove his way through the forest to the base of the cliffs, not hurrying, but determined. As he scanned the trees along his path, they called out to him, rustling—*danger*—but he ignored their voiceless pleas. Akemi was preoccupied and besides, he owed himself and the mission increased knowledge of this remarkable planet.

Arriving finally, Gordon gazed up at the rough cliffs, covered by leafless brambles outlined against a darkening sky. A line from a poem he learned in school floated through his mind. "The tangled bine stems scored the air like strings of broken lyres." Yes, it was easy to visualize those broken harp strings scratching at the atmosphere.

As soon as he took his first step onto the jagged cliffs, the sun disappeared. The sky's "spectre gray," just as the British poem described, filled the air with desolation. He moved faster.

Thorns clutched him as he climbed, forcing him to

jerk his limbs from the brambles. He passed fissures in the rocks where steam bubbled out with a fetid odor that made him gag. His breathing grew harsh.

Suddenly, Gordon was overwhelmed by a premonition of trouble. He must return to the base before nightfall. He started to turn, then stopped, forcing himself to disregard the feeling. He wouldn't take samples this time. Just one peek and he'd head back. Science demanded it.

Clawing and gasping the last steep yards to the top, Gordon leaned over the cliff to see what lay beyond.

Chapter Nine

Back at the base, Dmitri stared at a specimen of chocolate bark under his microscope. He tried to concentrate, but his mind strayed. What information could he possibly send back to the EEF? How could he couch his words into believable reports to Earth? His "Aunt Sonya" would be waiting. He could report the new navigation instruments had zeroed in on the only possible landing site as seen from space. He could describe the exhilaration he felt in the tingling air of this planet, but that was no secret. He would have to settle on describing the advanced instrumentation of *Frontier 2*. A few quick comments slipped in would have to do for this first call home. These he could disguise from the others while they would be available to prying eyes.

"Auntie" would not be interested in his growing warmth for his lab mate, Beyatriz Cardozo. The dark haired beauty still wore her magnificent tresses rolled into a twist on top of her head, pulling her skin so tight her black eyes dominated her face. Her thin nose, full lips and high cheekbones hinted at Gypsy blood. Bey was all business in the lab and sharply professional at the conference they had both attended, but the spark between them lit her gaze. He would never forget that symposium. When the meetings ended, they escaped from science and seriousness for one intimate night. His delight in loosening those dark waves until her silky hair fell to her shoulder blades was surpassed only by what followed. Heat and sex and laughing surrender. He sighed. *That night, and that woman…how wild and wonderful*. Would he ever experience such abandoned feelings again?

For a rare few moments, Dmitri's constantly worried look was replaced by a secret smile. The lab, the microscope, indeed the entire planet faded away as he relived the hours in that huge bed, sinking into fluffy pillows and even softer skin. The night table drawer filled with sex toys, and Bey eager to try every one. How they had enjoyed the tiny vibrator, the velvet handcuffs, the long strand of 'poppet' pearls. She was cloaked in a haunting, musky perfume straight out of the Arabian Nights. They had played and loved until dawn. He'd dreamed his way through the flight back home.

Had it really happened? Once he returned to cold, bleak Moscow, he convinced himself that fucking Bey, no—*loving* Bey was merely a wild dream of wish fulfillment, so powerful it had taken on a tactile reality. But there were so many explicit details! The feel of her satin skin. The perfume of her hair. The taste of her taut nipple as it tightened in his mouth. The intoxicating sounds of her excited breathing… Here on Nacre, he could believe again.

****

On patrol the day the wind rose, Lara wandered through the tent labs offering to help wherever a spare pair of hands was needed. She didn't bump into Gordon in any of the labs, nor had she observed him among the nearby trees or down by the lakeshore. As the hours passed, uneasiness filled her. Perhaps Tenn knew where Gordon was. She left the labs to search for the captain.

Reaching the spaceship, Lara found the door of *Frontier 2* open, Tenn at the controls. "Inspecting everything *again?"* she teased.

He looked up from the computer. "Constant vigilance, don'tcha know." He grinned, then sobered. "There's still too much we don't understand about this planet. That's why I've ordered spacesuits left on until the comet shows. More bodies to keep track of, and I don't like leaving the ship alone. Even Gordon has gone off somewhere."

"Just what I wanted to ask you. Where is he?" Lara leaned forward and kissed him lightly.

"Hey, you can do better than that." Tenn rose and pulled her closer, pressing her against him until their spacesuits rubbed together. "As your superior officer, I expect a proper salute." Their kiss grew deeper quickly, but they kept it short. With the comet due the next night, they would get their fill. Sex could wait.

"So," Lara asked, licking her lips as they parted. "You didn't send Gordon on an errand?"

"No. You saw Akemi and she was alone?"

"Yes, totally absorbed in what she found under her microscope."

"Where do you think he's gone?"

"I wonder if he went off to explore those ugly cliffs. They fascinated him on our earlier trip. I know he wanted more soil samples and was eager to see the other side of Paradise."

"Now that you mention it, I recall his suggesting an exploratory party. He shouldn't attempt to explore those cliffs on his own. They could be dangerous." Tenn frowned. "We'd better check it out."

"Right." The two grabbed their helmets and added their emergency packs. Both had learned to be wary of pitfalls surprising Earthmen in an unknown environment.

Pausing only to enter a quick report into the computer, Tenn set out with Lara beside him. As they passed the inflated pods, Jenny Duncan stepped out of one of the labs and held a small meteorite up to the sun. Blushing as if she'd been caught playing hooky, the scientist offered a sweet, satisfied smile, then arched her back and stretched. Her cheeks looked flushed. Sunlight gleamed through her hair, weaving a golden halo.

Dr. Stan stuck his head out, saw them, and popped back inside. A spot of hanky-panky in the lab? Lara wondered. That's what her mother called it, and the signs were there. A little prelude to the comet's arrival, perhaps.

The captain stopped to tell Jenny where they were heading. "Send out a search party if we're not back by dark," Lara added, joking but still serious.

Jenny looked intrigued, but merely nodded and waved.

The wind had picked up; as the comet drew closer, the air grew even more effervescent. The two quickened their pace. "We need to bring Gordon back before nightfall tomorrow." Lara worried aloud as they strode through the forest. The leaves on the trees surrounding them fluttered wildly, echoing her anxiety.

"Damn right," Tenn said. "We've got to be there together when the comet arrives. Otherwise, the crew will be mystified and unsettled. I could have briefed them, but I wanted each one to share the astounding feelings we underwent with our first experience."

"I agree. The improbability of what's happening will make it hard for them to cope, especially after all the lascivious hints we've dropped. Scientists won't want to accept what's happening as real. They'll convince themselves they're hallucinating."

"I can hardly wait to see their reactions when it finally sinks in." Tenn's step took an extra bounce.

Lara smirked. "Me, too. And, don't forget, Gordon wants to share this first experience with Akemi. He's talked about little else."

"We'll find him." Tenn's authority implemented his conviction. His positive tone comforted her. They lengthened their strides.

As soon as they reached the base of the cliffs, they felt the change in atmosphere. The heavy, gray air seemed an impenetrable curtain. *It's spooky,* Lara thought, conscious of the weight of her backpack. She hadn't noticed it before.

Tenn peered through the drifting fog and scrutinized the cliffs. "There are no visible paths to the top," he said, "but some of the bracken has been bent out of shape in a couple of places." He pointed them out, and Lara followed his finger.

"We'd better separate. The spots are close enough for one of us to holler to the other if we find Gordon."

"Or anything else," Lara whispered with a shiver.

"You okay?" He must have caught the tiny quaver in her voice.

Lara straightened. "A-O.K." With a smile and a salute, Tenn started up the right-hand break in the bracken. Lara began climbing the one on the left. As she pulled herself through the tangled brambles, their sharp thorns dug into her hands right through her gloves. She felt their sting but soldiered on. She smelled rot. Wrinkling her nose, she held her breath on passing the spot where the fetid steam escaped. Her eyes no longer followed Tenn as he climbed. The ascent required all her attention.

At last, she clawed her way to the summit. But before Lara could lift her head to peer over the top, a boot landed heavily on her grasping hand.

Chapter Ten

"Hey!" she yelled, twisting her head around. Gordon stood behind her, spacesuit torn and a wild look in his eyes. No longer whiskey brown, they had taken on the "spectre gray" of the surrounding air. He looked—Lara gulped as the word sprang into her mind—possessed.

Quickly, she threw off the notion. Her training took over. An unknown virus had most likely caused the transformation, not a demon. She'd overreacted, having read too many paranormal stories on the voyage.

"Gordon, it's me, Lara," she called out. "The captain and I came to find you. The comet is close. You must get back to Akemi!" She struggled to remove her hand from beneath his boot.

Those staring phantom eyes showed no sign of having heard anything but the name. "Akemi," he growled. "Yes, I'll take you here on the summit of my world." Ripping off her helmet, he dragged Lara's body to the very top before he fell upon her.

"Gordon, no!" she screamed, pushing futilely at his heavy frame. "This is Lara. Your co-pilot. Can't you see? *I'm not Akemi!*"

She knew he neither saw nor heard. Savagely, Gordon pawed at the Velcro straps of her spacesuit. "I'll take you here, break you here. Punish you here." His voice had changed, grown deeper, darker.

What had happened to the Gordon she knew? Lara batted at his hands, trying to push him off her. Something in the air had not only changed his eye color, but tripled his strength as well.

He had torn open her suit and was unfastening his own when a hand grabbed him by the collar. With a roar, he turned. In a flash Tenn landed a vicious blow to his chin.

Gordon's head snapped back, but he swung around with lightning speed and threw Tenn off him. Before Lara could crawl out from under he was back on top of her, pressing a large hand over her nose and mouth.

She couldn't breathe. Her blood pounded. As Gordon's body covered hers, she started to black out, dimly aware of Tenn attacking Gordon again. With a furious curse, he pulled him off her once more. Dazed, Lara panted, caught her breath as she watched the two men pummel each other. Scrambling to her feet, she grabbed her weapon, set it on stun and aimed at Gordon.

The two bodies rolled closer and closer to the edge of the cliff. Lara danced around them, trying to get a fix. She bit her lip. Adrenaline surged. They were about to roll over the edge to the far side when she pressed the trigger and fired.

The blast struck them both. Pushed backward, they continued to roll, faster and faster, down the familiar side of the cliff.

Lara screamed. No one was there to hear.

Heart thumping wildly, she hurried after them, sliding and slipping until she, too, was stopped by the bracken halfway down. She pulled herself back onto her feet and ran to them. The captain and Gordon were both out cold.

She paused, took a deep breath. Neither man looked in shape to get back to the base on his own, and she had no idea how long it would take for the stun effects to wear off. Glancing up, she saw her backpack lying close to the peak, its med kit inside. Lara swore.

Even though they had landed on the safe side of the cliff, they would perish if left there until she could return with help. She had to get them to the protection of the loving trees in the forest below. The trees possessed the power to revive and heal the stunned, battered men. She felt certain of it.

Puffing with exertion, Lara pushed and pulled, letting the two men roll short distances whenever the area was clear. Time passed. Dusk was closing in when she finally dragged the two bodies under a sheltering tree.

At the touch of chilled human flesh, the chocolate-like tree limbs moved. Two branches spread out and curled around the backs of both men. The twigs on the branches massaged their backs, and their eyes opened. *Thank Space.* She had been right. As she sat down beside them, Lara watched in astonishment. The men turned from the tree and embraced each other.

"Oh no!" she cried out, listening to caressing murmurs in masculine tones. These two, she was certain, were not destined to partake in a homosexual affair. Some men swung both ways, but she'd been in the Navy long enough to know her crewmates didn't fit the profile. The trees apparently didn't care which sex fertilized them or how the ejaculation came about. Lara's only option was to get between the two before their rubbing against each other went any further, and it grew too late to repair the damage.

When Tenn's and Gordon's lips parted in a noisy, popping kiss as they separated, Lara squeezed between them.

"Lara!" Tenn shouted.

"Akemi!" Gordon growled.

Both men began to pet her. Tenn kissed her tenderly, reaching inside her open space suit to fondle her breasts and tweak her nipples. As he nibbled his way down, Gordon opened the last of her pants tabs and pushed the sides apart. His mouth pressed against her, his tongue seeking entrance to what Akemi had referred to as 'the doorway to heaven.'

Tenn slid up once more, his teeth gliding over her tits as she reached for the Velcro tabs on his suit and pulled. She bent down, and his cock jutted out—right at her parted lips. As if it had a mind of its own, it plunged into her mouth, growing larger and harder as it scraped along her teeth. She began to pant. Down below, Gordon inched closer to his heart's desire.

As her lips slid up and down Tenn's dick, tightening the pressure, Lara stopped concentrating on her own pleasure to open her eyes and watch the two men. Tenn stared with glazed eyes at Gordon, too far gone in rising rapture to be aware of what he saw. Gordon, too, looked up from lapping at her clit to stare back unseeingly, lost in his fantasy.

She closed her eyes again, luxuriating in the feel of Tenn spurting inside her mouth while she shivered and trembled at the erotic touches making her ache with desire below. Her mind fractured as she gave herself to sensation. Lost in her magical world, she was barely conscious of the men sliding around to change places, of time passing. How she loved them both! She reached out to Gordon, squeezing his balls and tickling his ass, while below Tenn slid inside her still quivering pussy. She moaned, tightened her inner muscles, heard him gasp and move deeper inside her. He bent his head and nuzzled her breasts with every long stroke. All her senses were stimulated, and she was on fire.

"Oh well," Lara murmured as the loving mood of this planet overtook her, "I might as well relax and enjoy it."

Somehow, she found herself beneath both men, who were on their knees. Gordon flicked his fingers on her tits, and as they tightened he raised a breast to his mouth. Tenn swirled his tongue around her belly button. He moved two fingers inside her while his thumb played with her clitoris. As she crooned in pleasure, something felt different. Her eyes opened wide.

The tree had joined in the fun. Two limbs dropped down and slung around behind the men. Chocolate fingers, formed into circles, ringed their cocks and rubbed back and forth while tickling their assholes. Suddenly, she became conscious of feeling not only her own trembling tits and excited clitoris, but the pull and tug of two penises enveloped in rapture as well. Her sensitivity flared, and her entire body throbbed in response. She felt it all, and it was love—not just gratifying sex, but real love. Romantic love for her Captain, tender love for her teammate, and a totally new and fascinating love for her own body. Even though one man knew she was Lara and the other thought she was Akemi, their emotions entwined with hers.

Satisfaction. All knew it. They were three…and at the same time, they were one.

Their orgasms, held back as long as possible for the sheer pleasure of the almost…almost…right now…*yes*, feeling, crept up on them. In some glorious, magical way, she felt Gordon's surging blast of joy. She sensed Tenn's delicious creeping, building, bursting, on and on until he was claimed in bliss. And all the while Lara gave herself completely, opening like a rose, petal after petal, sensation piled upon sensation, until the flower revealed its heart in ripples of glowing colors, flaring and spreading over the three in a blanket of rainbow velvet. *Our own hot Fourth of July celebration,* she thought, when she was capable of thinking again. *Rockets bursting in air, oh yeah.*

Lara lost count of her own climaxes, couldn't recall how many the men shared with her and how many all of them shared with the loving assistance of the tree. She was struck with an astounding revelation. The poisons from the other side of the cliffs had paradoxically ignited a fantastic sexual fusion. *This remarkable planet continues to amaze me,* she told herself as she drifted at last into dreamland.

****

The tree under which they nestled gave them time for only a short nap. When they awoke, the men were themselves again, sated and happy, although Gordon looked mystified. "Where's Akemi?" he asked.

"Uh, she hurried back to camp to watch over her experiment," Lara improvised. "She's waiting for you there. We'd best get back as fast as we can. Tomorrow the comet is due, and the others will be worried if we're not there to supervise the initiation."

As they walked along, Lara turned to Tenn. "Up there at the summit, you saved me, Captain." She tried to make a joke of it. "From a fate worse than death."

His horror at the memory still showing, Tenn swallowed, then managed a low chuckle. "My mom used to read those books aloud sometimes, the old-fashioned ones with all the clichés. We kids got a giggle out of it."

"Really?"

"Yep, it was a family game. You should have been there, Lara. Happy times. The scenarios we came up with trying to imagine a fate that could be worse than death were hilarious. What crazy imaginations kids have."

"Like what?"

"Oh, to be sucked into a giant vacuum cleaner. Whirled around in a humongous washing machine. Squeezed in an elephant's trunk. Forced to eat liver."

"Sounds like you had a loving and challenging family."

He paused, looked into her eyes. "We lost my father when I was thirteen, and I kind of took over his role with my younger brother. Mom was wonderful. She understood what we were all going through, leaned on me when she had to. I grew up in a hurry but, looking back, I know I was one of the lucky ones."

"I see." SEAL material, there it was. She hadn't realized how deep his protectiveness went. They turned to see Gordon loping ahead of them, and Tenn lengthened his stride. "We'd better hurry and catch up."

"One last question before we get back, Tenn. Did you look over the top? I never had a chance."

"I guess that saved you," he said. "I took a quick

peek before I heard you yell. Felt my eyes changing for a nanosecond, but I scrambled down so quickly when I heard your panic that the effect hadn't time to take hold. At any rate, I know who and where we are."

"The tree cured you." She looked up into his eyes. The last of the cloudy haze covering the deep blue faded away as she watched. "Check it out on your computer."

"No time. We've got to hustle."

With a skip, Lara sped up. "What did you see? Were there any signs of life?"

"Nothing moved in my quick survey. I spotted some leafless, twisted trees dotting an arid landscape, and more of that dead wood littering the cliff. If there were any creatures hiding among it, they didn't show themselves."

"That's too bad…or is it?"

"Whatever, we're going to have to work out safeguards before we let anyone explore the other side."

"If it's a virus that got to Gordon, we'll begin right away to find an antidote." Nodding, they began to run, caught up with Gordon.

"What the hell happened today?" he asked. Tenn and Lara stared at him.

"How much can you remember?" she demanded.

"Not much. My head is still foggy. I finished my work at base early, so decided to explore the cliffs. It was a helluva climb to the top. But then I…" he paused, stuttered, "I c-can't quite remember what happened after I started d-down the other side."

Lara patted his arm. "Your memory will come back when the shock wears off. You attacked us at the top when we came to rescue you. Tenn fought with you, and I was forced to use the stun gun. Then you both went rolling back down until stopped by the brambles."

Gordon peered at them. "I attacked you? I don't believe it."

"Not only that." Tenn's tone was grim. "You thought Lara was Akemi."

"What!" he shouted. "Akemi is half your size, Lara, and has a long black braid. How could I make such a mistake?"

"Forget it. You weren't yourself. I had to scramble down after both of you when you started to roll. Dragged you over to the tree. Do you remember that?"

"No…not clearly. But I do know that when I awoke I felt damned good. The trees performed a miracle again. Shame Akemi had to hurry away."

Lara and Tenn passed each other knowing looks. Gordon believed his vision, and they wouldn't correct him. The three picked up their pace and hurried through the agitated forest, sighing with relief when they sighted the blue waters of the lake.

They reached the field medical lab, a model of scientific knowhow and efficiency. Dr. Stan insisted on whisking the captain, Lara and Gordon inside for a quick scan before they were allowed to address the group. He ordered their torn spacesuits preserved and all of Gordon's clothes sealed and examined for any signs of contamination. Bits of twigs, thorns from brambles, splashes of sap and flecks of soil were all trapped for dissection.

Then the four hurried outside to join the rest of the crew and prepare for the miracle of the planet. The next night the comet appeared directly above. As the scientists stared at each other, their forms took on a magical luminescence. Everyone began to glow. Shimmering fingers wiggled in front of their owner's faces, and both men and women laughed in delight.

Breaking away, Akemi ran over to Gordon. "What happened yesterday?" she asked.

Gordon looked at her strangely. Then he shrugged. "It's a long story. I'll save it for later—the comet will be passing any minute now, Akemi. We each need to find a tree."

Chapter Eleven

"Listen up," the captain called to the group. "It's time for the great experiment. Each of you choose a tree and sit down beneath its boughs. Try to relax your minds and let whatever happens happen. Don't fight it, and you'll have a life-altering experience."

The group fanned out, Tenn and Lara selecting the trees in front. Gordon herded the other four scientists to a middle row, while he and Akemi took the rear.

The comet swung closer. The humans relaxed in the tingling air. Leaves brushed their foreheads in a soothing caress, a subtle perfume permeated their nostrils, and, one by one, their glistening bodies began to slump. In a few moments, they were asleep. The alien trees repeated their loving ritual of the year before, caressing and stroking, sliding and squeezing—pleasuring their willing subjects in every way. With a beneficent alien technique, they wrapped each individual in a private cocoon of thrills and satisfaction.

Jenny was timid at first, slipping slowly into relaxation, bit by bit opening herself to joy beyond belief. Bey accepted the strangeness of the chocolate twigs with exuberance, leaping into the new and fabulous experience, shouting its magnificence aloud. Akemi's long braid had swung out to reach Gordon, and she hung onto the feeling of his tug on her scalp, aware of their togetherness, their rightness, even while blending happily with her tree.

Dmitri sank into his sensations quickly, having had much practice in fantasizing his pleasure. This was better than vodka. Stan wriggled under the tree's ministrations until he finally gave up fighting to enjoy the wonder. And wonder it was.

Tenn and Lara shared the thrills, knowing deeply how the other felt. Their emotions from their first time under the tree increased the joy of this second time. For each and all of them, the loving tension built and built until all reached the pinnacle, the exotic hours climaxing in eight gloriously intense orgasms.

The sheltering trees were once more fertilized. Soothing leaves of red and orange, pink and purple, drifted down to cover their new family in warmth. Sublimely sated, they fell asleep.

No work was accomplished the next day. Everyone was too busy discussing what had happened, some shy, others boastful, but all filled with a love toward each other that sprouted that night into a star-strewn orgy. Luxuriating in the soft sand, with the lake's gentle waves slapping on the shore in a soothing rhythm, and the breeze wafting the exotic scent of night-blooming blossoms, gleaming bodies marveled, chuckled, sighed, panted, and moaned, bathing in pleasure. Screams of delight mingled in the effervescent air with the purring sounds of soul-deep satisfaction. Each pair responded differently, yet they blended together in a pattern of moving grace. Sensitized bodies touched each other everywhere with wonder, laughing as the thrills raced on and on through their circle and back around again. Their final cries of joy evolved into a rapturous tune sung by the wind. And the wind, dancing through the whispering leaves, carried it everywhere.

****

The next day the comet passed, leaving behind an afterglow of happiness. Postponing any discussion of how to handle the revelations when back on Earth, Tenn and Gordon set the scientists to analyzing the fetid air that had drifted out of fissures in the cliffs. Before they began their return journey, they had to find answers for their superiors at home. Much hung in the balance—not only opportunities, but careers, reputations, scientific miracles and, especially, the preservation of a wondrous planet.

Doctors Jenny and Stan, working with the newest model of mini electron microscope to unearth plant DNA, reported their findings to the crew. "From what we've been able to discover from everyone's contributions," Dr. Stan said, "once a race lived here with humanoid qualities similar to ours. Their chemical structure produced a binome that linked them with the plant life on Nacre. Then, about fifty thousand years ago, Nacre's comet threw off some material in its tail that landed on the far side of the planet. If we were able to explore that side—and someday we will—I feel certain we would find a large crater.

"Our data suggests the asteroid landing on Nacre broke apart. Each meteorite contained molecules that united with the DNA in the plants it came into contact with and became a parasite, absorbing all the moisture within its living host. The atmosphere gradually grew poisonous. Strange mutations occurred. One virus attacks the nervous system of humans and causes dangerous, even lethal hallucinations."

Noting their troubled expressions, he went on.

"Fortunately, the air carrying this mutated microbe is too heavy to rise above the cliffs, thus preserving this side of the planet in its pristine state. This condition has remained inviolate for thousands of years, but there is no guarantee that another asteroid won't land and destroy the balance. We need to find a way to detach the good DNA from its contaminated mutation and return the entire planet to Eden."

"How long do you think it will take to find a 'cure'?" Lara asked.

"I can only guess," he replied. "Our research in microbial diversity has been advancing at fantastic speed ever since we found the hook into the DNA double helix. A specially equipped laboratory back on Earth, linked to a satellite laboratory here on Nacre, might find the solution by the comet's next passing.

"This may be too optimistic. Still, given the rate science is advancing, and the enthusiasm of all who've worked on the project, I feel it's a strong possibility."

As he spoke, Lara glanced over at the trees. The twittering leaves seemed to nod in agreement.

The doctor stepped down and Captain Tenn took over. "We have another week here on Nacre before *Frontier 2* heads back to Earth. Let's make the most of it. Remember, when you communicate with loved ones back home, both from here and when you've returned, the biggest miracle of this planet can only be alluded to. On our first visit, Gordon, Lara, and I made a pact to allow only those in the top ranks of authority know all our findings. It would be too easy for inconsiderate, profit-hungry mavericks to destroy what we found here through carelessness—or greed."

"Or deliberately for power," Dimitri added. "The

EEF would kill to know about this planet, but killing would be the result." He turned toward Beyatriz and spoke softly. "No matter what happens to me, I cannot allow it." Exhaling deeply, Dmitri released a weight he had been carrying for years. He and Bey would find a way to safeguard his mother.

"Have I the solemn promise of everyone on this expedition," the captain continued, "to honor our vow that this information remains classified?"

The group turned and looked at each other. Gordon and Akemi shouted yes, and *hai,* then turned to hug and kiss.

Jenny gazed at Stan, filled with admiration…and something more. "You've handled the scientific explanation magnificently," she whispered to him. "I want us to return and explore Nacre undisturbed…and our own feelings as well."

Bey smiled dreamily. "This is a world of wonder. I want another chance for more, more, more!"

To Lara and Tenn's delight, the dedicated scientists not only nodded, but spontaneously linked hands as they pledged to preserve what Lara classified as "our new family." Their enthusiasm was infectious. His tension gone, Tenn felt lightheaded.

Turning to Lara, he picked her up and swung her around. Within seconds, Gordon was twirling Akemi, Doctor Stan was hugging Jenny, while Professors Dmitri and Beyatriz executed a fiery Flamenco tango, staring into each other's eyes as they danced around the field. Bey began to tango first, tapping her feet and beckoning to Dmitri with curling finger and provocative smile. For a moment he hesitated, but then jumped in, stamping his feet to her rhythm and clapping as loud as he could.

Lara clung to Tenn, hugging him tightly. He kissed the top of her head as they whirled around. She forgot the doubts, forgot her terror at the cliff top, forgot Gordon holding her down, intent on rape. Ugly dreams might follow, but in another world.

Yes, they had claimed this paradise and would preserve it. Their children would know its wonders. Nuzzling into Tenn's broad chest, Lara swore she heard enchanted music echoing through the forest. The fluttering leaves kept the beat, and it synced with the rhythm of her heart.

Part Three
The Third Expedition

Chapter Twelve

Another perfect day in San Diego, California. Ocean breezes blew, sudden gusts dissolving the smog that drifted down from Los Angeles. Here at Coronado, swimmers dotted the beaches and the sun shone in a clear sky. The cool breeze petted sunbathers, stroked bikinied bodies. On such a rare day, this corner of Earth felt a little bit like Nacre.

And that was the trouble.

"I want to go, I want to go," Lara chanted, the soft wind ruffling the hairs on her arms. She stood shin deep in the ocean and let the foaming waves splash as high as the maternity swimsuit she wore.

A muscled arm circled her waist. "Laralove, you know it's impossible." Tenn's exasperation leaked out. "I've given up my command of *Frontier 3* just to be with you when the baby is born."

She drooped. "I know." She kicked-splashed the salty water into his face, then gave up her petulance and turned in his arm to kiss him. "A baby is what we wanted. We decided after the last expedition to take our Lifemate vows, and I'm glad we did. But it's hard!" Her last words came out as a wail.

"Speaking of hard," Tenn rubbed against her, pressing salty lips to hers. She licked them, and his mouth slid around to nibble at the spot below her ear that always aroused her. "Let's take a quickie break, so

I can ease your pain." His rumbling voice vibrated on her skin and tickled.

"Another one of your excellent ideas, Admiral, Sir." Lara's voice turned husky. The moisture she felt didn't come from her wet bathing suit.

Holding hands, they raced back to the house and opened the door to the kitchen. Lips still on hers, Tenn untied the three knots that held up her swimsuit. He pushed aside the breakfast dishes, splashing leftover coffee as he lifted Lara onto the table. Nuzzling her neck, he slid his lips down to press a kiss upon her belly. "Hi, Junior," he murmured. "I think we broke the record getting back here."

"Mmm. What I'd expect from a SEAL responding to a booty call." Grinning, Lara swung her legs up and locked her ankles around Tenn's waist. "Ooh, that's good," she mumbled as he dropped his trunks and slid inside her. Her body tingled deliciously, inside and out. She wriggled closer, and they rocked together. "So good."

Their tender coupling lasted five strokes before speeding up, flesh slapping, till it ended in panting moans and sighs of satisfaction. A magic moment passed as they sank into themselves, wrapped around each other, the only sounds the distant rolling waves.

Fucking with Tenn gets better and better, Lara thought as she felt herself thrumming inside. *I picked the perfect mate. It's even more enjoyable now that I'm pregnant. Didn't expect that.* With the hand that wasn't petting Ten's abs, she drew feathery circles around her stomach. *Wonder if the baby feels my happiness, too…*

With a long sigh and a big grin, Tenn turned and lifted her head. Cupping her face, he kissed her deeply.

"Space, but we're good together, Laralove."

"You're reading my mind again. Think it's because we don't need a condom now?"

"That helps, but it's ninety percent us. We fit. We should finish every meal with this dessert."

Lara smiled. "What the French would call a *digestive.*"

He nibbled at her fingers. "That word makes me want to gobble you up again."

She could feel his reluctance to stop, but her back began to complain. "Maybe next time we can keep my hair out of the toast crumbs."

Chagrinned, he moved off her and began to clear the table. "I'll pile the dishes into the sink, since you take so long to dress."

She stuck out her tongue at him but didn't argue, knowing work called. "Ready in ten."

As they headed for the base, he tried again to comfort her for missing *Frontier 3*. "Don't feel too bad, Lara. We'll be in touch with the crew daily once they arrive, so we'll be nominally in charge. Meanwhile, we'll both be training recruits for space travel here at Coronado. And during your six weeks of maternity leave, you can fancy up our condo. You'll enjoy that."

"I know," she grumbled. "I'd like to turn it into a home at last, instead of a waystation between deployments. And I'll probably be a doting mother as soon as the infant is put in my arms. I'm going to feed her myself, so you'll have to take turns at my breasts." Her eyes gleamed as she taunted him.

"We'll see about that. Fair's fair…and I'm bigger."

She snickered. A riotous picture of Tenn suckling one breast and the baby the other, their matching blonde curls tickling her, flashed through her mind. She would tell him one day.

"Don't forget," he continued, "we'll be navigating *Frontier 4*. We've a lot to learn about the starships being designed for the gravity-wave launch. The engineers will have worked out all the kinks by then, but we'll need to practice new methods of propulsion and control. The time will fly by before you know it."

"You're right." Lara squeezed Tenn's thigh. "Pinching spacetime—it still boggles the mind. How thrilling to return to Nacre in the magical *Frontier 4*." Her eyes filled with wonder.

Tenn nodded. "Not magic. Just science getting ahead of us again. I agree it's mind-blowing."

"I'm still having trouble imagining it. To think Einstein was right all along, centuries ago."

"He blazed the trail, but our astrophysicists have turned the amazing idea into twenty-second century transportation. And we'll be among the first to use it. Thank goodness your parents agreed to take the baby for a while when he's a year old."

"I'm not sure taking up my folks' offer is the best deal for her. Mom and Dad can be pretty strict. Dad's so…military. My brothers are off somewhere, and Mom loses herself on the Internet. Computers are her real children. I must have griped about it to you before." At his nod she continued, "I was left to grow up by myself."

"That's harsh."

"I know, but realistic. I love my parents, but your mother might do a better job of nurturing her."

"Him."

"Her."

"We could check the sonogram?"

"Not that again… I want to be surprised."

"Okay, okay. My mom would love to take on the challenge. Another boy to raise! She could call him Percy, after Shelley. He was another poet she admired."

"Ugh. There's another 'fate worse than death' to add to your collection." Lara giggled. "And if it's a girl…Desdemona?"

"Nope. Othello's too tragic, no Desdemona. And not Ophelia, either. Poor girl has a horrid end."

"She drowned, didn't she?" Lara shuddered. "How about Portia! There's a heroine worth her mettle."

"Sounds like a car. The kid'll be teased to tears. Shakespeare's out. We'll have to look elsewhere for inspiration."

"Agreed." Ignoring the air conditioning, Lara opened the car window, breathed in the salty air. "I hope our choice of guardianship won't start a war between the families."

"I doubt it. Some battles are necessary, but we'll find a way around this one. Whoever we choose, you're clever enough to figure out the perfect reason."

"So I get to be the bad guy?"

Tenn smirked.

"At least we have four more months to figure out how to prepare them for our decision. Maybe I'll have twins and we can give them one each!"

He glared at her. "Not funny, Lieutenant."

Lara laughed, remembering how she'd worried about Tenn being as overbearing as her brothers. What a white dwarf she'd been, afraid to recognize the tender loving man inside her buff SEAL. Thank Space she'd learned better. 'Course they still argued, but she'd never been as close to another person. A bit scary, how well he understood her.

"Meanwhile," she changed the subject, "teaching classes to new recruits will be an…invigorating change, don't you think?"

"Despite your sarcasm," Tenn said, "I'm actually looking forward to it. I'll get an advanced taste of what I can look forward to when I'm past the age to command missions."

"What a horrible prospect."

He placed a hand over the one Lara rested on his thigh. "You'll still be my gorgeous playmate, even when you're ninety! If we ever slow down, we'll hop on a flight to Nacre and take a refresher course."

"Now that's a brilliant idea!"

Chapter Thirteen

Gordon, too, had elected to forego this mission. He was getting to know Akemi's son, Kouji, and enjoyed playing with the youngster. Space, he'd already been defeated twice in Orbiting Dirks and Laser Dragons. Convincing Akemi to give Kouji a sister kept distracting him from the game. Not surprising. Working on the baby notion was pure consuming pleasure.

They both still dreamed of returning to Nacre. If this current mission could figure out a way to reverse the asteroid's fallout, end the fear of plague, and return the planet to its pristine state, he'd like to settle there. Nacre would be a great steppingstone toward exploring another star system in the galaxy. When he mentioned this to Akemi, a look of speculation filled her eyes. "Nacre would be a fine place to raise children, too," she said.

The other scientists from the second expedition couldn't hide their eagerness to return. For the last two years, Drs. Stan Lieder and Jenny Duncan had been employed at CERN, the nuclear research center in Switzerland where the giant neutrino smasher was housed. The grad school lovers were finally reunited, forgetting their long separation for further training, followed by the mind-numbing stress of high-powered jobs. Since they began to work together, a lot of teasing followed their obvious devotion. But they put up with it. Stan had mastered the art of misunderstanding, while Jenny had perfected the raising one eyebrow silent response. Even so, they'd finally been goaded into moving up the date of their Lifemate vows a month ago.

Their work now was so intense, the hours so grueling, the new mates longed for the refreshing air of Nacre—their "Garden of Eden." They'd even chosen anagrams of the planet's name, Crane and Caren, for their children to come. In Nacre's tingling, pheromone-rich atmosphere, they counted on conceiving one of each sex. Their unspoken pact to try at every possible opportunity was agreed upon with a wink, a Nacre handshake, and a quick roll in the bubble wrap lying in a nearby storage room. A co-worker passing by heard the pops and grinned. Their friends always knew where not to find them!

Elsewhere on Earth, Professor Dmitri Petrov fought the urge to lose himself in vodka as he waited anxiously for flight day, praying that nothing would go wrong. Back in Brazil, astronaut Beyatriz Cardozo skydived to reel in her wild impatience.

Dmitri and Bey intensified their longing through daily texting and nightly calls, even wangling their way onto scientific conferences around the globe. Although Dmitri longed to propose to Bey, his orders to spy for the East Europe Federation held him back. On Nacre, disobeying the order seemed the way to go, but his resolve fizzled in the frigid atmosphere of home. Such a life could not be offered to this splendid woman. Yet, when they were together, nothing seemed impossible. Perhaps on Nacre they would find a way. The loving trees would lead them to a solution.

Both Stan Lieder and Beyatriz Cardozo were licensed space pilots as well as scientific experts, so the remaining two seats in *Frontier 3* were saved for the exploration robots, R-Crick and R-Watson, named for the Nobel Prize winners who discovered the DNA Double Helix a few centuries ago. How that amazing discovery had speeded the change in everyone's lives!

These latest Artificial Intelligence robots were programmed to continue learning. On the long journey, the male crew members spent their free time teaching R-C and R-W new tricks—including expressions better left on Earth. Jenny and Bey protested at first, but soon gave up and joined in. The robots' vocabularies expanded rapidly, their understanding of usage at a slower pace, and their unsolicited remarks added chuckles to the sober trip. Soon R-Crick was calling for wine o'clock, R-Watson insisting on beer. Their mechanical smiles of satisfaction when lubricant was added to their joints lightened the boredom of the journey.

One day, Stan and Jenny taught them how to play poker. They were quick learners, even absorbing human competitiveness. By the time *Frontier 3* landed on Nacre's sandy shore, R-Crick and R-Watson had won the crews' salaries for the entire year.

The forest's foliage had grown lush since their last visit, but all else appeared unchanged. Labs and sleeping quarters were quickly erected, and communications established with Earth. The crew set to work, their anticipation high. On this trip, they had a week to prepare for the comet's return.

Equipping the robots for exploration and sampling duties, the team led them to the base of the cliffs. On their first outing, R-Crick held the scoop, R-Watson the plastic bags. As soon as the foul air reached them, red and yellow lights began to blink on the robots' chests. "The air is unclean," R-C said in his treble monotone. R-W's flat baritone added, "Smells like shit."

"You—" *cough* "—taught them well." Jenny choked on her laughter.

"*Merde!*" came from R-C's voice box.

"Dmitri's touch," Stan chuckled.

"That's it," Bey said, exasperated. "You've got their intelligence up to junior high level. Let's get the experiment started."

Settling under a tree, Jenny and Bey watched as Stan and Dmitri led the robots to the paths that still showed faintly among the flattened brambles on the cliff face.

"Climb to the top," Stan ordered them, "and head down the other side. R-Watson, pick up samples of dead tree leaves, twigs of bracken, and pieces of bark. Check for meteor debris and collect any small meteorites. Deposit your samples in these bags and seal them. R-Crick, keep your camera running and film the panorama. Then dig up three ounces of dirt and place your sample in this larger bag. Put your scoop inside and seal it. When you have collected everything, be sure the seals are intact and return with them to base."

"A-O.K." R-Crick's mechanical voice squeaked.

"Yes, sir, asshole," rumbled R-Watson.

The women looked at each other and shook their heads, hiding their grins. As they turned back, R-C's treble rang out once more. "Boys will be boys."

"They've got parrots in their brain circuits," Jenny said as the chuckling men smacked palms in a high five. With one last look, they headed back to camp.

As soon as they escaped the bad air, Nacre's effervescence invigorated them once more. The four sang a raucous chorus of 'Anchors Aweigh' as they marched along. Though the Navy tune got lost along the way, the leaves on the trees they passed swayed with the rhythm of the song.

"I'm glad our trees aren't critics," Stan muttered to Dmitri. "But the song's words are so tame. We need a rousing booty call."

"Wait till the comet arrives," he replied. "Someone is certain to be inspired then. Or…we could ask the robots to invent new lyrics."

"That could be a hoot. Let's do it." Snickering, the men shared the complicated finger grip they'd named the Nacre Handshake.

****

As soon as they reached base camp, the scientists continued their attempts to isolate the genome causing the plants on the far side to wither and die. They waited for the robots to return with samples, humming to themselves as their work ran smoothly. Stan glanced over at Jenny, caught her eye, and winked. *We're so lucky to spend our days doing what we love.*

"I saw that," Bey called out. "Keep your mind on your microscope, Doctor."

Red-faced, Stan gave her a third finger salute. Both women laughed.

****

By late afternoon, R-Crick and R-Watson had tramped back to camp. Dust from the terrain on the far side clung to their boots. Wherever they stepped, leaves along the path shriveled and fell, but no human was there to notice.

As soon as they returned, the robots were sent to the decontamination chamber and hosed down with a powerful chemical solution. Their containers, too, were isolated until cleared of microbes, and the samples divided among the four scientists. R-C and R-W trotted back and forth fetching and carrying. Absorbed in analyzing the specimens, the scientists were oblivious to the world around them.

The comet approached. The wind picked up, ruffling the surface of the lake and blowing dead leaves into camp.

Jenny stepped outside for a breath of invigorating air. Hearing the crunch of dried leaves underfoot, she stared down. *Great Galaxy! What have we done?* She grew dizzy as shock drained the blood from her head.

With shaking fingers, she paged one of the robots from the mike in her ear and ordered a large specimen bag delivered to her immediately.

Within seconds, R-Crick was back with the evidence bag. Croaking out the order through her blocked throat, Jenny pointed. For a few shivering moments, she watched him gather a bagful of withered leaves. Then she called Stan, her voice breaking as she explained the situation. "Approach with caution," Jenny told him. "It may not be safe."

The doctor hurried out, bringing R-Watson along. He reached for Jenny's hand, but she backed away. "We can't take a chance," she said, her voice husky, her eyes wide with fright. Helpless, they watched the robots fill the bags near the camp.

"Shall I alert the others?" she asked.

"First, let's see the extent of the damage," Stan

replied. The two followed the trail back, robots in the lead picking up debris. As they entered the forest and saw the denuded trees along the path, Jenny couldn't hold back a howl of dismay.

Stan reached out to comfort her, but lowered his hand before touching. His glance took in the devastation as far as his eyes could see. Forcing himself to become the scientist first, he pushed his anxiety about Jenny to the back of his mind. "Thank goodness the blight has affected only the trees along the path. We've got to stop it from spreading."

They raced back to camp. As they were telling the others what had occurred, Earth called. The captain's voice came through their headphones from the SEAL's home base at Catalina. From Stan's greeting alone, Tenn picked up on his anxiety. "What happened?"

"There's been a mishap," Stan said, trying to control the tremor in his voice. He took a deep breath, then snapped out quick, sharp details. Picking at a cuticle until it bled, Jenny waited her turn, then blurted out her description of the devastation.

The pause between transmissions from Earth to Nacre lasted seconds longer than usual.

At last Tenn spoke. "I picked the finest, most intuitive scientists we had for this mission. I'm counting on you to find the antidote for this blight, even if you don't yet know the cause. We have to stop the destruction. I'll check the labs here at home and get back to you on what's been discovered from the samples we brought back."

Lara stood beside Tenn, squeezing his shoulder. "It's horrible but we trust you, Stan, Jenny, Dmitri, Beyatri…" Her encouraging words faded away.

****

Back on Earth, Lara and Tenn drove from the base to the medical labs functioning twenty-four/seven in San Diego. Her hand lay on his thigh. Though immersed in their own thoughts, they comforted each other through touch. At that hour, the traffic was light. The captain drove fast but with a steady hand. Through her tension, Lara felt the baby kick. With a start, she placed her other hand on her stomach while she squeezed Tenn's thigh in excitement.

She pulled back so she wouldn't disrupt his concentration, but he knew without words. "What's the matter?"

She couldn't hold in a grin. "The baby just kicked me."

For a moment, he took his eyes off the road to smile at her. "That must be a good omen. He wants to come out and grow up on Nacre."

"She sure does." Visions of naked, panting bodies, of wild, wonderful sex in the tingling air, filled her head. Tenn's sharp turn into the lab's parking lot jerked her back to Earth. Worry returned, and the glowing planet vanished from Lara's mind.

Chapter Fourteen

The four scientists worked feverishly through the nights, taking turns sleeping in two-hour shifts. The comet grew nearer. Around three o'clock on the second night, Jenny's head snapped up. She stared at her fellow researchers.

"What are you doing?" she screamed, slapping Stan's hands away from the slide he was slipping under the microscope.

He dropped it, turned to her. One look at her dull gray eyes, and he signaled the robots to come at once. "Jenny. Stop!" he called as she began sweeping equipment to the floor. "Contain her!" he ordered the robots. "Isolate her in sick bay and see that she touches nothing but the sheets on the bed."

From the far end of the lab, Bey and Dmitri heard the commotion and hurried over. They saw the frantic look Stan aimed at his lifemate. Stunned, they watched as tears begin to trickle down his cheeks.

"What's happened?"

"I don't know yet." Stan's agonized gaze dropped to the fragments on the lab floor, then rose to watch Jenny being led away, fighting the robots and cursing.

"Jenny has caught the virus… I don't know how." He tried to pull himself together as the communications button lit up. Earth was calling back. Tapping heels were audible in the background, hurrying across a hard lab floor.

"Report," Tenn ordered.

"The situation has accelerated," Dmitri spoke first. "It is bad. Dr. Duncan-Lieder started acting strange a few minutes ago. She is shouting and smashing the lab equipment."

"Is Lieder there?"

"Yes, I'm here." Stan spoke dully into the communication device.

"Does Jenny look any different?" Lara asked.

"Her eyes," he responded. "They're dull and gray, as if a film covered them."

Beyatriz interrupted him. "What happened to the shoes she was wearing when she crunched the dead leaves?"

"Damn." Stan smacked his fist against the table. "We never thought to decontaminate them." He gestured, and Dmitri ordered R-Watson to dispose of Jenny's boots.

"How are you progressing with the antidote?"

This time Stan was quick to answer. "I'd begun to get positive reactions to my chemical solution when Jenny knocked my slides off the counter. I'll start again immediately."

"Our labs in San Diego have come up with some formulas to try," Tenn said. "They should be filling your screen now."

"Sir, we need to find the antidote fast!"

"I know." The captain's concern was loud and clear. "You can do it, Stan. You're driven, and you love Jenny. I trust you to end this crisis."

"Is everyone else still healthy?" Lara cut in.

"Affirmative."

"And Jenny has been put in quarantine?"

"Yes, R-Crick is guarding her and R-Watson is on his way."

"Everyone, put your troubles behind you for tonight, and get back to work." Tenn's voice rang out, calm but positive. "We'll keep testing here. As soon as we know more, I'll contact you. Try out those formulas I just sent *now*. There's no time to lose." Earth clicked off.

After a stunned moment, the scientists swept up the debris and hurried back to their posts. The lab counters were sprayed with an anti-bacterial solvent, and testing continued.

"Perhaps," Dmitri ventured as he and Bey began to work on the formulas, "when the comet arrives it will erase the disease. Certainly, strange things happen when it passes over." He turned toward Stan. "The comet will help," he assured him, and signaled a thumbs-up.

Returning from dropping Jenny's shoes into the decontamination chamber, R-Watson joined his robot partner in keeping the patient quiet. Inside the isolation room, robotic arms fed her intravenously with a nutrient solution. R-W raised her bed as needed and R-C fed her frequent drinks of water.

Jenny had lucid moments when she asked how the others were progressing with the antidote, then she fell back and began thrashing again. Her eye color switched back and forth with these episodes, the dull gray signifying the onset of another mindless period. As the comet drew closer, her sane moments increased. Occasionally, her green eyes peeked through the gray haze.

They waited. After an hour, Dmitri suggested they try the nutrient solution on the withered trees along the path. If it helped the trees, they'd know how to go forward with the experiment. He and Bey left, taking a robot to carry the equipment. They inoculated all the affected trees. By the time they reached the end of the path and returned to base, the first trees had begun to lift their branches. Small buds appeared where others had fallen off.

The two smacked hands then leaned over the path and hugged. "The trees have an affinity for substances that keep humans healthy," Bey remarked.

"Indeed," responded Dmitri, "and the comet's closeness aids in their recovery." They moved nearer to kiss when they heard a cry. Separating, the two broke into a run.

****

Stan came racing out of the lab. "I've found it!" he shouted. "A combination of chemicals that destroys the genome. The cells are once more absorbing water."

"Are you certain?" Bey's excitement morphed into anxiety. "Is it safe to inoculate Jenny?"

Squaring his shoulders, the doctor stared her down. "It has to be. Jenny is my lifemate. I can't lose her!"

They hurried to the infirmary. Bey bit her knuckle. Dmitri gritted his teeth. Stan kept blinking as they peered through the treated glass. A mechanical arm poured the new ingredients into the container of nourishing fluid. Then they waited. Watched. Fidgeted.

Time passed. The comet drew closer.

Even though the air grew fizzier, not much penetrated the sealed lab. Beyatriz began to nod, Dmitri slumped, but Stan didn't remove his anxious eyes from his mate.

The minutes rolled by. Dmitri shook himself awake. "Should we try something else?" The words had hardly left his mouth when Jenny opened her eyes, clear and spring-leaf green. She saw the others watching her and smiled.

"Hey, Gang," she called out, "had you all scared, didn't I? Stan dearest, is it really you?"

Stan looked at his lifemate, his eyes filled with unshed tears. "Yes, it's really me. Your nightmare is over."

She shuddered. "That describes it. As I started to go under, I remember I was terrified. Then everything went black. Sure am grateful you pulled me out of it. Is the virus all gone?" At their nods she added, "Hurry up and get me out of here."

She threw off the blanket covering her, walked to the radiating shower, then picked up a sterilized lab outfit and dressed. Her resilience amazed them. Jenny didn't appear weak at all. Had the comet given her strength?

The moment she stepped out, Stan grabbed her and hugged her breathless. They stared at each other, the air sizzling with their emotion. He ran his hands over her cheeks, then rested them on her temples as if he could verify that Jenny was really here. His Jenny.

She reached up and ruffled his hair. "Oh, Stan…"

"I can see your energy has returned, love. You certainly got out of that room fast. How are you feeling?"

She rubbed against him, not answering, just lifted her head from his hold and landed a quick kiss on the corner of his mouth. Bey and Dmitri slipped out.

Kissing her eyelids, her cheek, her temple, Stan started drawing circles on her scalp. She shivered and fell into his touch.

"Let's get out of here." Stan interlaced his fingers with hers and dragged her forward. "When I saw those green eyes light up and go brilliant, I flipped. I wanted you so badly! But you need fresh air. Nacre will finish the cure. Come on. It's time we found a tree."

Chapter Fifteen

The four scientists hurried to the forest. Relief and anticipation sent their feet flying. The bright light of the comet bathed them in a midsummer glow. Once again, they glittered. Bey reached out and moved her glistening arm to finger-draw hearts in the air. Like smoke, they glowed, sending out sparkles as they faded away.

Each chose the tree favored on the last visit. Jenny and Bey kissed the sweet chocolate bark. They glanced back at the men and deliberately licked their lips. Stan and Dmitri grinned and thrust their hips toward the women in an age-old male response. Then they smacked the branches they had leaned on before in familiar greeting. The element of surprise was gone this time, but their anticipation had more than doubled.

The wind grew stronger. Red and yellow, orange and purple leaves brushed their faces, soothing them to sleep. The light grew brighter, and the branches started to sway. Fingerlike twigs opened the four space suits and began to caress warm bodies. Sighs of delicious arousal whispered through the forest.

Despite having been gone for two years, the trees remembered their favorite sensory stimulation spots. Both women and men shivered as the caresses began. Back of their necks… Bey's insides leaped as the thrill slid through her. Beneath their ears… Jenny dissolved in delight. Under their arms… Both men felt their cocks expand and grow hard. Between their toes… Dmitri bit his tongue in excitement. Circling their navels… Abs jolted. Tiny quakes as chocolate fingers tickled their way down four backbones to the crevices below and probed the trembling hot spots.

All panted to slow down their climb to the peak. They were touched, stroked, tickled. A breeze, passing over their naked bodies, ruffled hair and brushed tits, heightening carnal delights as they gasped their pleasure. Dew dripped, landing on nipples as they tightened and tingled. The spicy perfume of Nacre's air enveloped them. Chocolate finger-twigs petted and pinched. Four people shivered and sighed, forgetting to breathe. And then came the final, ecstatic moment, the amazing climax to a fabulous day. Jenny screamed with joy while Bey cried out, "Aaaaaaah." Stan groaned his release. Dmitri's last thought as he collapsed, *Hot Galaxy. What a way to go!*

When they awoke at daylight, they plunged into the lake, splashing, swimming, floating, enjoying their bodies, and anticipating the night when they would pair off.

By lunchtime, they had returned to their duties— titrating, filtering, and filling vials of the antidote for the dangerous genome. They packed the solutions with extra care for their return to Earth.

That night, by the shimmering blue lake, Jenny and Stan licked each other all over, lapping up the brandied chocolate taste left on their skin. Beyatriz and Dmitri loved each other uninhibitedly and with pure wicked glee, fighting each other to be on top, twisting around for a pleasurable sixty-nine where they could devour each other to their heart's content.

The communication channel to Earth had been left open, and Lara and Tenn, stimulated by the squeals and moans they heard, and having just learned that they were expecting twins, shared their voluptuous movements on the beach at Catalina. They ended tonight's encounter with a run into the ocean. "Here," Tenn murmured into her hair as he slid inside Lara one last time that night, "your big belly doesn't get in the way." She turned to punch him, but he ducked them both and diddled her under the waves.

Behind a nearby dune, Akemi and Gordon joined in the loving, murmuring of luscious peaches and rock hard stems of jade, whispering poetry in tongue-dampened ears as they coupled sinuously, writhing around each other, slick with sweat.

Once again in Nacre heaven, all responded with age-old motions and brand new emotions. Sticky with the feel and taste and touch of sex, each couple glued together and basked in satisfied lust and—even more precious and rare—requited love. Need called, and it was answered.

****

The next morning, as the comet dipped over the horizon, the four people on Nacre began to pack up the lab. Dmitri debated sending word to "Auntie" about the antidote. No, he would keep that news a secret. Instead, he would tell Auntie about new meteorites found that contained nuggets of gold. Speculation about fortunes to be made would absorb the EEF authorities and give him breathing space.

When they had gathered their personal belongings, Jenny looked around. "Where's R-Crick and R-

Watson?"

"Space!" Stan exclaimed. "We forgot about them. They must still be in the decontamination chamber." Dropping everything, the four ran.

Stan unlocked the door, and they peered in. Jenny's mouth dropped open at the vision in front of her. Dmitri whistled in astonishment. Bey's eyelids rose so high, her pupils resembled capital O's. Stan stared, speechless.

The robots lay on the floor in pieces. Chunks of plastic and titanium were strewn about.

"What the hell happened?" Dimitri queried. Shaking his head, Stan sputtered, torn between frustration and laughter.

Jenny and Bey stepped inside for a closer look. The voice boxes still nestled inside the robots' skulls. "Can you talk?" Jenny asked R-Crick.

"Yes, we can." R-Crick squeaked. "But R-Watson started it."

"Did not." They spun around as the deep voice of R-W responded. "Until you returned," he intoned, his voice more guttural than usual, "we decided to play poker. When the simple game you taught us grew boring, we looked into our memory banks for other versions."

"So," Stan asked, "what has that got to do with your disassembling each other?"

"We can explain," said R-Watson.

In his higher pitched voice R-Crick added, "We found strip poker. We both lost."

****

When their giggles and guffaws stopped, the scientists hastily reassembled the robots. "I hope they never look up the word 'sex' in their memory banks," Bey whispered to Dmitri as they returned to their pods to continue packing. "Space knows what would happen then."

"Or 'eroticism.' What would they make of that?" The leaves in the nearest trees picked up on Dmitri's laughter, flapping hard enough to make the air buzz.

Sliding the lab equipment and the team's duffle bags on an inflated pallet sled, the group progressed to *Frontier 3*. In the morning, they would deflate their sleeping quarters, the last job before returning to Earth. As the robots marched to the space ship, two voice boxes began a new booty call.

"Space anchors aweigh, my crew, space anchors aweigh,

Farewell to Nacre' brew, we launch at break of day day day day.

On our next flight in space
Drink to loving trees,
Nowhere else is there a base
That goes all out to please.
Sex two three four
Sex two three four…
Yes we want more
Yes we want more…

"Told you they could do it," Stan said as they settled the robots into their berths in the space ship and strapped them down. "Bet they come up with a raunchier second verse." As the group locked the ship and returned to the forest, the sound of singing gradually faded. All was quiet except for the whispering breeze. This last night of love on Nacre was only for the humans—and the trees.

And what a night it was! Communication channels with Earth were left open once more, so that Lara and Tenn, Akemi and Gordon, could join in the final orgy *in absentia*.

The air hummed with unearthly music as all loved one another. Tentatively at first, they reached out. Minds and spirits hurtled through space to join the magic circle. At every touch their bodies responded, thrills radiating between and among them. Nipples quivered and firmed, cocks stretched and grew hard, balls tightened. All entrances to the warm bodies relaxed and spread open, throbbing with expectations. Thought vanished. Emotions, freed, took over, growing deeper, hungrier, increasing in intensity until, in one fiery moment—for each person and for all as one—they reached across the stars to the ultimate beauty of transcendence.

In some mysterious way, the trees shared their exalted state, bathing everyone in a sheen of radiance, making everything perfect. This was a night of pleasure and unity never to be forgotten.

While the humans slept, the branches swayed in frenzied abandon to the music of the cosmos. Then the comet passed on, and all grew quiet.

In the morning, the four on Nacre held hands and did a happy dance around their own part of the forest. Already, shoots of green with a rainbow of colored buds in all the hot shades were working their way through the soil to the sunshine. Then Stan, Dmitri, Jenny, and Bey took a quick swim and donned their space suits.

Stan overheard the two women talking, and walked over to listen. "It was wonderfully wicked," Bey said, hugging Jenny.

"Mmhmm, so naughty but nice," Jenny squeezed her in return.

"I'm surprised at your word choice." Stan stepped closer. "Naughty? Wicked? Do either of you feel any guilt for what you did these last nights?"

"No, indeed. Absolutely not." They shook their heads vigorously.

"Then it looks like we'll have to redefine those terms," he said, trying to keep a straight face. "Apparently, you can take humans away from Earth, but you can't take all of Earth's teachings away from the humans."

"Agreed." Dmitri strolled over to catch the last of the discussion. "Nacre will have to work on retraining our people, once they settle here."

"Well, if the jobs they did on us and our predecessors are examples of their capabilities," Jenny said, "Nacre and its comet are up to the challenge."

"Aren't we lucky," Bey echoed the sentiment. "When this wonderful planet is made secure, I want to be among the first colonists."

"Happy days," came from Jenny. "Fulfilling in every sense." Her words echoed and settled provocatively in each mind. Blowing kisses, they waved to the trees and headed back to the space ship. Once inside, the crew lowered their visors and checked on the resting robots. Their singing had wound down. The silence of space crept in. Dmitri tested the controls, and the door slid shut.

Watching on their screens as the ship leaped into the unknown, Jenny turned to Stan. "Look at the trees. Can't you feel their satisfaction coming to us in waves?"

"Can't beat ours," he spoke into the mouthpiece. "I think they're already awaiting the arrival of *Frontier 4.*"

"The real wonder," Bey added, "is that this planet makes a perfect stepping stone for further exploration of our galaxy." Inside her helmet, she grinned. "Who knows? Maybe next time we'll meet aliens. If they turn out to be as affectionate as our trees, we'll have opened a new universe of experience—all kinds of creatures living together in slippery satisfied love."

"Wow!" Jenny responded. "I like that idea." She smiled at Stan's back. "Is it possible we can be so lucky again?"

"Who knows? That's where the suspense lies!" As *Frontier 3* plunged into hyperspace, Bey's exciting words were drowned out by the sounds of singing. The robots had awakened. To the raucous chorus of "Space Anchors Awayyyyyy. Sex two three four, Yes we want more…"

They headed for home.

Part Four
The Final Expedition

Chapter Sixteen

"Holy quasars!"

Fourteen-year-old Kouji Lee spotted the weird vessel and stared. Where were the sleek, rigid designs of *Frontier* spaceships *1*, *2*, and *3*? As if having skidded down a black hole and been vomited out, the ship resembled a gelatinous mass. Tethered to the space station, it undulated in front of his astonished eyes—an amorphous figure eight dancing with a shark.

He and his stepfather, Gordon, had rocketed up to the space station a day ahead of the others. They checked on the equipment and personal necessities needed until the supply ship arrived, including—Kouji wrinkled his nose—diapers. Along with two intelligent robots, eight adults and five children were changing their lives. They would pioneer the first settlement on Nacre. Once above the atmosphere, the passengers could board the unlikely vehicle.

After nine years of experimenting, scientists and engineers had finally discovered the jellylike substance with the strength to carry a load. It could hitch onto a gravity wave and accurately pinch Spacetime, reaching the far side of the galaxy in nanoseconds. The new propulsion system would shoot the settlers to their destination almost instantaneously.

Hyperspace, which used light waves for propulsion, would send the robotic supply ship racing across the solar system, but the human brain had linked itself with gravity.

The Spacetime pinch had at last been manipulated into a feasible means of long distance travel. The strange, slithery vehicle, laughingly called *Frontier 4*, was currently attached to the space station in a cage of titanium fibers. It would soon fling the first colonists into another dimension, returning them to ordinary Spacetime once it reached its destination.

Commodore Gordon Lee trained for this flight, along with Captain/Admiral Tenn James, Lieutenant Lara Stone, and the rest of the earlier crews, but he still found this new way of reaching the stars incomprehensible. Had puny man really conquered the universe? He looked at his son, sharing the wonder. *Holy Quasars, indeed!*

****

A howling infant greeted Gordon and Kouji the next morning as the passengers in the docked capsule crossed over to the space station. Sobbing seven-month-old Caren and her whimpering two-year-old brother Crane were carried aboard by Doctors Stan and Jenny. Lara, the first one out, grabbed Jenny's free hand for support. It was unusual to see the sunny scientist frowning. Was she questioning the wisdom of taking the children to Nacre? She and Stan had agreed the shining planet would offer them a healthier, happier life, but Lara could see the worry lines between Jenny's eyes had deepened.

Stan looked troubled, too. Was he uneasy about the virus returning? Did he question if he was up to the challenge of banishing sickness from their new home? In his place, she would be. Like Tenn, Stan quietly radiated confidence. But as medical doctor for the entire settlement, he was faced with an awesome job. Perhaps it was the finality of takeoff day having arrived at last that darkened his eyes.

It must have been grueling traveling with two fussing children. They had been given a calming draught before takeoff, but hours passed before the delivery rocket finally shot into space. That was followed by the shock of the blast, and no amount of practice had prepared them for the huge jolt. No spoonful of medicine could temper the body's reaction. Even cherry-flavored rocketpops hadn't helped.

Tenn's and Lara's eight-year-old twins were cranky, too. Gryf and Tedra bickered, their high voices penetrating everyone's space helmets in the limited quarters. The colonists and crew of the space station milled about, crowded as kippers, while two dark blonde heads threaded with glints of red slivered around legs, bumping into everyone. Mission leaders Tenn, Lara, and Gordon worked around their pulsing headaches to re-ignite the group's enthusiasm, even enlisting a disgruntled Kouji to amuse the younger children. Throughout the din, Lara remained calm on the outside, but inwardly she was anxious. Would she find everything the same on Nacre? The loving as joyous? Did her paradise still exist? Unsettling questions kept circling her brain.

****

Gordon cornered Tenn. The captain could sense his co-pilot was plagued with far-reaching concerns. The wrinkled frown between his eyes called out for assurance. What if another large meteor fell? The colony could not survive another virus. Were the armed

115

drones surrounding Nacre capable of destroying an asteroid without jarring the comet from its orbit?

Wishing he could pop an analgesic or three, the captain reassured his crewmate. He still relived his shock upon seeing Nacre in the news. Their secret was out for all to see. A media feeding frenzy followed, and the crew had gone into hiding—until today. Tenn knew it was too recent for greedy Earth bandits to interfere with their launch, but could aliens have broken through the drone blockade and invaded the planet? *What if their brains are more advanced than ours?* He ground his back teeth. *Can our robots react instantly? Have they been programmed to think of retaliation?*

At the launch site, the dismantled robots, inflatable pods, and other indispensable items were stowed inside the weird ship's "hold." Once the passengers were strapped into *Frontier 4*, Lara collapsed onto the nearest bench. For a few minutes, she could relax. Specialized stabilizers brought about a sensation of normalcy, quelling any dizziness. Unhappily, her timeout didn't last. They needed to hitch onto a gravity wave, but only the computers could predict the moment it would pass. As the minutes dragged on, faces revealed the doubts and fears that continued to float on the currents of air.

Dmitri couldn't stop thinking of the EEF. He had not received new directions before this flight. Were his spying orders lost in the regime's latest *coup d'état?* It sounded too good to be true. He'd been unable to reach his mother before taking off, but Olga Petrovna's brilliant mind had resonated with his in the past. He knew she was safe and would find a way to help him clear his conscience. He must. It was his only chance for a future with Beyatriz.

Bey, meanwhile, bit her nails, the queasiness inside her nothing like the anticipation she felt before skydiving. Dmitri had been ignoring her. What was wrong? Where had the trust gone? She itched for the fabulous sex they shared, wanted more. But what if…*bah*. She squirmed in her seat. This was no time to feel insecure. She would solve the problem on Nacre.

As Bey reached this decision, Akemi leaned over and rested her gloved hand on Kouji's. She wondered if her son would forget his heritage. Seeing Gordon bond with the boy pleased her, but someday Kouji might wish to return to Earth. What would happen then?

Kouji moved his other hand to cover his mother's. His grin spread wide. "Hot galaxy! We're really doing this! Colonizing a new world!" He turned toward the twins and smacked their hands in a high five, the old gesture standing fast through the generations. Then he twisted his ring phone to the selfie camera and texted his best friend back home.

****

Ever since being chosen for this mission, Lara had argued with Tenn about a possible invasion of Nacre. What damage a greedy group from Earth could do! And what if aggressive beings approached from another planet—what danger might they bring? Frightening possibilities hung over Lara, shaping her dreams. In the dead of night, black clouds of huge-headed, tentacled aliens weighted her down.

She fought to hide her distress, but she hated concealing her thoughts from Tenn. It had already created a rift in their relationship, and that scared her. Growing up trying to be Wonder Woman in a Navy home, Lara leaned toward force, whereas Tenn, the SEAL with a poet's name, called for peace. Wasn't that ironic? They could only agree on caution and stealth in dealing with what might come, but after that...

Now, however, was no time for fractious feelings. She would respect the captain's authority, stifle the side of her nature that would widen the rift. It was time to clear the air, remind the others of the pleasures to be found on their wondrous planet.

As they waited for the Spacetime pinch, Lara and Tenn filled the passengers' earphones with tales, reminding them of velvety sand by a lake of crystalline blue, of whispering leaves reflected in shades of red and violet, of tingling air caressing the skin, urging the walker to bounce and skip. Hints of carnal desires fulfilled in spectacular ways aroused the adults, while the children were promised magical new adventures. They were still talking when science's latest "miracle" occurred—they found themselves on the sunny shores of Nacre.

Chapter Seventeen

The first step onto their new homeland brightened the colonists' spirits. Lifting the visors on their helmets, they breathed in the effervescent air and spun around, stretching and sniffing. Kouji and the twins began to bounce, the slight difference in gravity adding a spring to their steps. Even two-year-old Crane and seven-month-old Caren laughed, wriggling and kicking in their parents' grip.

The adults hurried to set up the recently developed inflatable rooms. Each of the dozen pods they'd brought of a new material strong enough to resist a Category 6 hurricane, would inflate to a comfortable two-bedroom suite, or a large laboratory. With one touch, the pods sprang open like an antique umbrella and fastened to the ground in the blink of a photon. Robotics expert Dmitri activated R-Crick2 and R-Watson2. He and Gordon supervised the robots' construction of the labs. The heavy scientific equipment, sent ahead by drone ships, was already waiting, undisturbed, at the landing site.

"Home sweet home," announced high-pitched R-C2 as soon as his voice box activated.

"Home is where the heart is," came R-W2's rumbling reply.

"Who taught them all the clichés?" Lara asked, exasperated. "Are we never to escape?"

The others laughed. "Wait till they really get going," Tenn teased. "Bound to be more surprises. Relax and enjoy them."

Jenny snickered. These androids had been programmed to elevate moods, and they blended with Nacre's invigorating air, restoring the group's energy. Space labs and scientific equipment were set up to the rhythm of the robots' tenor and baritone, mingling off key. Their haunting refrain came from long, long ago. "You and me we sweat and strain, bodies all achin' and wracked with pain…"

"Some wag on Earth had a great time programming them," Stan called out to Jenny as he helped haul medical equipment. "Must have found the Diamond Oldies list… Say, was it you?"

Standing on the sidelines with Caren in her arms and Crane's hand held tightly in her grip, she smiled and blew him a kiss. Her doubts about the move had vanished in the champagne air. Abandoning his own insecurities, Stan returned the loving smile. He detoured to drop a slobbery smack on her lips before moving on.

Twisting her neck to watch them, Lara sighed in relief. She had noticed their hesitations and been concerned, but her psychotherapist's expertise was not yet called for. The atmosphere of Nacre had already solved one problem.

It wasn't long before the colonists were ready to establish communications with Earth. A ground crew of scientists and engineers heard their reports via photon tunneling and wormhole transmission. Shouts of joy rose above the noise of backslapping on Earth, while the pioneers on Nacre hugged each other and clapped for themselves.

Brief personal calls followed. Tenn and Lara assured the grandparents of the twins' safety, Gryf piping up that space flight was 'tast,' the latest tweenybop praise. Jenny and Stan checked in with colleagues at CERN and heard the latest news on photon smashing. Bey wowed her skydiving friends with a quick, excited description of the miraculous flight.

Akemi assured her parents in Japan that she and Kouji were happy to be here with Gordon. The teen agreed, shouting "stupendous," his favorite new word. Gordon tried out a Japanese phrase of greeting Akemi had taught him, and laughter emanated across the vast distance.

At last, Dmitri reached his mother at their dacha in the country. Olga Petrovna spoke rapidly in a little known local dialect, spelling out a command code she had just perfected for the robots. It would enable him to reach her without going through official channels. He memorized it even as she spoke.

Finally, the Lieder babies were fed and put down for an afternoon nap with the robots as babysitters. Everyone else assembled by the blue waters of the lake. Heated Instapaks of southern fried chicken with mashed potatoes and candied carrots were passed around, along with packets of beer and soda. Hot coffee bubbled in an inflated urn, adding the rich aroma of home. Last came grapefruit-sized chocolate chip cookies to celebrate their first meal on Nacre.

"Good, but no *empanadas*." Bey sighed.

"And no *blinis* or *borscht*," Dmitri added, a twinkle in his eye.

"It won't be long before we're importing goodies from home," Tenn said.

Lara grinned. "Always the optimist, Captain. Aren't we lucky, guys, to have him as our leader?"

Nods and shouts of "Hear, hear" and "super, rad" followed.

"And don't forget, the ultimate goodies are right here on Nacre." Bey dipped her head toward the trees.

Dreamy smiles and wicked grins responded to her remark. As if a wind had sprung up, the colorful leaves swayed and whispered back.

****

Already, the comet could be seen with the naked eye. In a week, it would pass over the planet to work its magic. While the adults talked quietly among themselves, Kouji and the twins, having nicknamed the androids Cricket and Deep Throat—soon shortened to DT—ran back and forth, playing hide and seek through the colorful forest. Tedra tired of the game first. "Let's each pick a color and see who can stack the biggest pile!" she shouted, already pulling down red leaves.

Watching, Kouji turned his ring and recorded her on video. The robots appeared, one carrying baby Caren, the other balancing Crane on his shoulders.

"You must not damage the trees," DT admonished in his gravelly voice.

"Oh stuff." Tedra tugged at the infant in Cricket's arms. "Can I have the baby?"

"You do not own this baby, Tedra Stone-James."

"Space! I mean can I hold the baby?"

"I may give her to you if you promise to be careful. Those are her mother's orders."

"Okay, snitchmouth." Tedra sat down under a tree.

"We'll have a tea party," she told the child. Some old videos she'd salvaged before they deteriorated had given her the idea. Picking only four leaves—one red, one orange, one purple, and one yellow—she declared them the plates. "And here are some pebbles for the cups."

The baby flung out her arms and gurgled, then reached for a pebble with chubby-fingered dexterity. After a few trials, it landed on the leaf. Drooling, she clapped her hands.

"Cricket," Tedra said, you are the teapot. "Can you bubble and hiss?"

The robot stood beside her. His mechanical voice droned, "I am not a teapot, Tedra Stone-James." Giggling, Kouji kept the ring camera rolling.

"Do you know the meaning of *pretend*?"

"The word is in my memory banks."

"Well, look in there and see if you can make a noise like a teapot."

After a moment's pause, a cranking, whistling sound issued from Cricket's voice box. The baby chortled. Tedra laughed so hard she rolled halfway over with Caren in her lap, catching herself before the android could take the baby back.

Gryf ran over to see what was happening. He caught on quickly to his twin's game. "You be the pourer, DT," Gryf ordered. "Make a sound like water running." A hissing sound emerged from the other robot.

Clicking off his camera ring, Kouji grabbed Crane and swung him around. "We'll be the cookies," he shouted. "Crunch crunch."

"Yay, crunchcrunchcrunchcrunchcrunch." The

teenager and the two-year old danced around the tree and fell over, laughing even louder when fallen leaves crunch-crunched beneath them.

With a sly grin, Gryf snapped their picture. He'd beam it through a wormhole to his friends back on Earth.

****

When the sun began to slip behind the distant hills, Jenny and Stan said goodnight. Taking the sleepy children from the robots, they strolled back to their quarters. After tucking them in, they left a robot babysitting and walked to the edge of the forest. Arm in arm they gazed at the darkened sky, ablaze with stars. A soft breeze ruffled their hair. They breathed deeply of the intoxicating air and smiled—the intimate, knowing smile they'd kept for each other since their schooldays.

Walking farther into the woods, they came upon a small clearing. As the trees whispered a siren song, Stan reached out for Jenny. She flowed into his arms, matching his instant arousal with moistened lips, damp silk between her thighs. With no words needed, they undressed each other and clung, skin to skin, excitement growing as they rubbed in all the right places.

"We did it, we're finally here," Stan crooned, pulling her on top of him.

"Yes, we did, and it feels right for our bodies to celebrate this first night under alien stars." Jenny's flesh had taken on the pearly essence of Nacre's moon.

Stan lapped at her breasts as if they were twin bowls of cream. He lifted her till she straddled him. As she stroked his cock, it grew under her hand, swelling until its only rightful place was deep inside her. She gasped as he slid home, riding him faster and faster until, as one, they melted into the newly rising moon.

****

Back at the campsite, the twins were allowed to play games in bed for another hour. With older brother privileges, Kouji kicked around a soccer ball, joining Gordon and Tenn in a practice game. Lara and Akemi acted as goalposts, goading the players and cheering them on until the solar lights on their helmets lost the battle to the dark.

Dmitri didn't join the game. Observing his morose bearing, Bey tugged at his arm, urging him to walk with her around the lake. He could see she was determined to find out what was wrong. As they sauntered along the sandy shore, not touching, Dmitri's averted eyes mirrored his struggle to keep Bey at a distance. It was tough going—fighting both the magnetic sexuality of the planet and his own need to pull her closer.

Finally, with an exasperated huff, Bey grabbed his hand and twined her fingers with his. "Won't you tell me what's troubling you?" she asked, squeezing Dmitri's palm hard enough to force a response.

Shadows crossed the lake, but he continued to look away. From the corner of his eye, he noticed her foot tapping.

Still without facing her, he let the wind carry his words. "My government wants me to spy, Bey. I am a traitor. You cannot fall in love with a traitor." His drooping shoulders lowered farther into a slump.

Her toe stopped moving. "Dmitri, what have you done?"

"Very little, so far," he protested, recognizing the accusation in her tone. "I sent them the coordinates of our landing site, but they could have discovered those for themselves."

"So you aren't compromised yet? Not beyond repair?"

"No. But they will not leave me alone. Even light-years away, they have me trapped. My mother still lives near Moscow…" His words trailed away.

She reached out. With a curse, he knew she felt the tremor beneath her touch. "Surely," she said, "they wouldn't harm Olga Petrovna—the Queen of Robotics?"

Dmitri turned at last and stared at her. She flushed. "I did not mean it to sound sarcastic. My words were sincere." Bey leaned into him. "Your mother is an EEF treasure. All Earth would be up in arms if something happened to Professor Petrovna. Ask anyone. From general to housemate, her robots are indispensable."

"You don't understand," he said, his voice laden with weariness. "The leaders have only insinuated, as is their way. But they delay the arrival of necessary parts, hack into streaming photon transmissions, disrupt incoming texts. Annoyances…they never end. Once, a shipment of my mother's caviar was delayed for three months, out of spite, I'm sure. When the box arrived, the contents were spoiled. What a stench!"

"Oh, my." Bey's nostrils twitched.

"The new leaders are uncertain where her loyalty lies, so they constantly test her. Last year, after we shared several vodkas, she confessed to feeling like a mink waiting for the trap to shut on her cage."

The two started walking again, Dmitri sullen. He could sense Beyatriz concentrating fiercely, but she came up with nothing. They were almost back at the campsite when Dmitri stopped and bit his lip. "I have just remembered. When we connected with Earth earlier, Mama slipped me a code for programming our robots here on Nacre. My anxiety was such, I forgot about it."

Bey turned so quickly, she bumped into him. "Access to a secret channel known only to your mother?" He nodded.

Grabbing both his arms, she pulled him toward her. "Are you certain the code will work?"

"I cannot answer your question, but the androids will know. They are clever and learn fast." He paused. "With their help, perhaps we can find a way to submit false information without getting caught."

They stared at each other. Slowly, recognition dawned. The corners of Dmitri's mouth turned up, and he stood taller. Bey smiled so brightly she rivaled the sun's reflection. As the last streak faded on the darkening water, their confidence returned. Dmitri basked in its glow.

Hand in hand, they ran back to camp. All was quiet when they arrived, the playing field deserted. Bey looked about, stifling a yawn. "First thing tomorrow morning?" she suggested.

"Indeed. It has been an exhausting day. To think only this morning we were hundreds of light-years from here. It is time to sleep." Dmitri reached for Bey and kissed her gently.

"Not so fast. We may be tired, but today's thrills aren't over." She threw her arms around him and hugged him tightly. Their impetuous kiss turned passionate in an instant. Open-mouthed, they tasted each other hungrily, breaking through any remaining barriers. Dmitri pulled Bey even closer to him, taking a deep breath of her alluring, musky scent. He lifted her tall form, aligning them until the bulge in his pants pressed against the vee between her thighs. She swung her legs around him, melding into his embrace.

The lovers pulled apart before weak knees dropped them to the ground. Still panting, they gazed at each other, offering unspoken promises. As breath returned, they looked up at the sky—the comet was drawing closer. "Until tomorrow," Bey said, twining her fingers with his for one last squeeze.

"Until tomorrow." He squeezed back, a vision flashing through his mind of their wild night in Rio and the hotel room filled with sex toys. He could see his silk tie circling her wrists as he tickled her palm. It was rolled up in a corner of his bottom desk drawer at home, still redolent of her unique scent. When his spirits were low, as they frequently were in Moscow, he would take it out and bury his nose in her fragrance…

****

The next morning they slurped a quick breakfast and hurried to the lab pods, only to find the robots were gone. "Cricket and DT went hiking through the forest with the children," Jenny told them. "They took a picnic basket, but should be back by dinnertime." She peered at them. "You seem mighty disappointed…"

"Uh, no, everything is fine," Bey blurted and turned away.

Unable to restrain a sigh, Dmitri added, "No problem. We will find them later."

Chapter Eighteen

With the picnic debris collected and stashed into the basket, the children and robots ambled back to base. "Cricket," said Kouji, skipping backward as he remained in front of the group, "What happens when the comet arrives?"

"The comet does not arrive, Kouji Harada-Lee. It passes over the planet and circles the sun. It flies over Nacre every six months."

"Our sun?"

"We do not own the sun."

Kouji let out a long sigh. "Do you mean the sun that warms Nacre or the sun that warms our Earth?"

"You are funning me. The sun of Earth is so far away the comet would not return in an Earthling's lifetime."

By now, the twins had caught up with Kouji. "Cricket, does something bad happen when the comet crosses over us? Is that why we have to stay in the children's pod with you and DT?"

"I do not know what you mean, Tedra Stone-James. What is bad? I only know that the planet renews itself whenever the comet passes over."

Tedra looked at Gryf. He shrugged.

But Kouji was full of ideas and speculations. He turned to DT. "Do you have sex in your memory banks?" he asked, running his tongue along his lips.

Gryf and Tedra looked at each other, then scrunched their noses. "That again?" they shouted and ran on ahead.

"They're so young." Kouji gave the androids a conspiratorial smile. "Will you answer my question?"

"The word is there, Kouji," said DT's deep voice. "All living creatures, animal and vegetable, use sex for regeneration."

"Vegetable... Yes, I learned about that in school. The bee pollinating the flower and stuff. But it's not what I mean."

"What is your question, Kouji san?"

"Uh...do our trees here on Nacre have vegetable sex? There aren't any bees here. And is it different for humans?"

"Humans do not perform vegetable sex."

Scratching his head, Kouji tried a different approach. "What do the trees have to do with the humans when they regenerate?"

"My memory banks have not been programmed for this question," came DT's gravelly voice. "I will ask the captain to program it in for me."

"And I will ask Commodore Lee," Cricket's treble added.

"Better not," came the hasty reply. "You two will get me into hot plasma."

"Where is this hot plasma?" Cricket inquired. "We will protect you from it."

"Never mind," Kouji hurried to say. "A lot of help you two are!"

"Thank you," the robots chorused.

Kouji giggled. "I'll see what I can learn on the web. It must be there, I just need to find the right search engine. But if that doesn't work, it's back to eavesdropping."

"I have no explanation for how to drop eaves, Kouji-san. Can I drop something else for you?"

"Space! Now you're learning how to make jokes! You two are too much."

"Too much what?"

Kouji threw up his hands. "Forget I ever asked." He turned and raced back to base, a sly grin parting his lips.

****

Dmitri and Bey cornered the two robots as they lumbered into camp carrying the younger children. Caren slept in the leaf-lined picnic basket Cricket held, rocking it back and forth as he walked. Crane rode on DT's shoulders, lids drooping but fighting naptime.

The moment the androids were free, Dmitri called them to his sleeping pod where Bey waited, chewing her nails. The unexpected morning sex had been delicious, but with so much on their minds, the lazy mating ended too soon. Only the odor of sexual pleasure lingered.

Dmitri fed his mother's code into the robots' computer banks, careful to list the symbols in the proper sequence. Once again, Olga Petrovna had designed a way to defy the authorities. Her crafty ploy offered misinformation on the number of ore-rich meteorites collected. Bogus reports of exotic elements discovered on Nacre would appear at intervals in "Aunt Sonya's" wormhole text, interspersed with fictional accounts of serums being developed from native tree saps. The robots were capable of making the data so plausible none would ever be doubted.

As Dmitri fed his orders into the computer memory banks, he suddenly laughed. Mamuchka never failed him. Cricket and DT were programmed to hold off communicating until information from Nacre was called for, thus assuring that messages would arrive infrequently. Each report would recommend holding out for additional material before taking steps. That should do the trick.

"Yes!" Raising his fist into the air, Dmitri turned to Bey, grinned, and dismissed the robots. "Let's go for a swim."

"Great idea. I need some cool water lapping over my body. All that clever planning has me sweating."

Her sideways glance kicked up his pulse. She extended her hand, as if to fan herself, but Dmitri grabbed it and pulled her to him. He leaned into the spot between her neck and shoulder, sniffing. "You exude a tantalizing scent, Bey—dewy petals on a camellia as the sun rises." Her low laugh was stifled as he nipped at the sensitive nerve, caught her shiver, and kissed his way around to the hollow at her throat. He felt her heart beating faster. Sliding down to drop a noisy kiss between her breasts, he dragged her away. "Let's get wet."

She smiled at his *double entendre* and followed.

They strolled around the lake until a bend hid them from view. Stripping, they dashed into the buoyant water and floated, Bey between Dmitri's legs, her hands stroking from his knees to his ankles, rubbing the hairs the wrong way before soothing them smooth.

Dmitri scratched at her scalp, idly twisting strands of ebony hair into corkscrews as he let the hot sun and cool breeze lull him. His trance was broken by Bey's sudden dive. She pulled him under, and in a nanosecond their passion returned. They fought each other, popping up for air, then plunging again. He pulled her against him as she locked her ankles behind his back. Gasping for air, they popped up to the surface, breathed deeply, then sank down again. Their heartbeats pounded like drumbeats, faster and louder, cymbals clashing until they shot to the surface.

Before their climax underwater could drown them, the lake's buoyancy pushed them back up. Panting and laughing, tasting their salty skin, breathing the fresh air laced with sex, they lay on the sand. "It was-*gasp*-just like skydiving." Bey laid her head on his stomach. "Fantastic fucking matches the thrill."

"Mmm." Dmitri ran his fingers through her long dark hair, separating the wet strands. "I'll settle for diving into you. Biggest thrill of all. No parachute needed…"

Chapter Nineteen

While the baby slept on in her basket sitting on the lab counter, timeout for resting was over, and the androids were once again sent to supervise the other children.

Lara and Tenn used their free hour to rush back to their pod, strip, step into the shower they'd rigged, and lose themselves in slippery, sudsy pleasure. Surely, no one expected them to remain celibate until the comet arrived! They scrubbed and tickled, slipping in and out of each other's embrace. Sliding in, sliding out, and touching, touching, touching. All the intensity of their sexual feelings for each other had returned with the force of their first encounter on Nacre. And how good it was!

"Ooh, ooh, ooh, that's… I love it I love it," Lara chanted in Tenn's ear as he soaped her breasts, weighing them in his hands while a fingernail scratched her tits. He enjoyed it especially when she soaped him back, squeezing his balls, then running a soapy finger up the crack behind, wiggling in and tickling there. Work breaks on Nacre certainly differed from coffee breaks back on Earth.

****

Returning to the compound's open area, the robots found it abandoned. Cricket and DT took off in different directions to look for the runaways.

During the short time they had waited for their lifelike chaperones, the twins badgered Kouji to take them to the cliffs. "We'll be careful," Tedra promised.

"We just want to see them up close," added Gryf.

"No, I can't. We were warned never to climb them." Kouji's stance mimicked his long-suffering parent to perfection. He knew he got it right when they continued to plead.

"We won't, we won't," Gryf promised. "We just want to see why they're so different from cliffs on earth. Why are the 'rents so scared we'll go near them?"

"I don't know," Kouji said, "but something mysterious is going on there. Something dangerous." He scrutinized the twins, but they kept their innocent expressions. "Okay, we'll go and take a quick look, but don't get too close. Remember, I'm leader. You've got to obey me to stay safe."

"Space promise," the twins said, holding their ring finger down while touching thumb to pinkie and crossing the other two fingers. Lagging behind them and keeping unusually silent, little Crane tried to match the strange finger ritual. His short fingers wouldn't bend right. Stamping his feet, he gave up at last and ran after the older children.

They meandered through the forest, imaginations fired up, shouting their guesses about the danger lying in wait on the far side of the cliffs.

"Dragons!"

"Vampires!"

"Poisonous snakes!"

"Two headed aliens—with green skin!"

"And tentacles!"

Masking their glee at participating in a scary adventure, they dramatized their fears with exaggerated shudders. When they arrived at the base of the cliffs, however, the sun disappeared. The sky turned gray, the air heavy. Their anticipation faded.

Tedra stared at the dried bracken clumping in ghostly shapes along the cliff's steep wall. She shivered. "Maybe we should head back?"

Relieved that he wasn't the first to mention it, Kouji snorted. "I told you so. This is a horrible place." His voice softened. "Let's go back to base and hunt down the robots. We can tease them some more. Bet they can tell us lots of things if we ask the right questions."

Kouji and the twins turned to head back, just as little Crane caught up with them. "I'm gonna clima cliff," he shouted, his running start heaving him halfway up the narrow path before the others could react.

"Space!" Kouji shook his head. "I'll be blackholed for this gig. You two stay here." He shook his finger at the twins. "Stay. I'll get him." Yelling at the child to return, he set off after Crane.

Kouji caught up with the two-year-old at the very top. He grabbed at the child's overalls, barely hanging onto a strap. Crane's small head was still below the cliff, but the teen came to a gasping halt as he breathed in a lungful of bad air. His eyes glazed over. Crane tried to wriggle from his grasp.

Far below, the twins watched in amazement as Kouji yanked the boy to the ground and pushed him hard. The child screamed as he began slipping down the cliff. As he rolled and flailed, a furious howl emanated from Kouji himself. The raw sound, mingled with Crane's panicked scream, echoed back and forth among the boulders.

The twins cried out. "Kooj," Tedra screamed. "What are you doing?"

Gryf shook his fist. "Stop!" he yelled.

Scratched and bruised, sobs mixed with screaming, Crane tumbled down. Near the base Gryf and Tedra ran forward. They reached out, but the hurtling body landed on top of them, knocking them backward.

As they pulled themselves up, Tedra lifted a sobbing Crane in her skinny arms. She backed away. Gryf turned to face the apparition moving inexorably toward him. For a moment, he stood his ground, but Kouji was no longer the young friend and leader they knew. Gryf gaped at the inhuman grimace distorting Kouji's face. He, too, tried to back away, but the teen's bared teeth and deadly stare scared him into immobility.

Tugging at thick strands of black hair caught in the brambles as he clumped his way down the cliff, Kouji yanked hard, leaving long tresses behind, but he didn't react to the pain. "I am going to grind you up," he bellowed. "I will crunch your bones. No one will escape me."

Crane shrieked, beginning to bawl again, his voice so hoarse by now it was more cough than cry. Tedra held him tighter. Biting her lower lip till it bled, she kept backing off, while Gryf searched frantically for anything to use as a weapon. There was nothing, not even a big stick.

With a loud roar, Kouji reached them. Backhanding Gryf, he tore Crane from Tedra's arms and threw the child to the ground.

"No!" the twins yelled as Kouji ripped off Crane's overalls. Still shouting, they pounded on Kouji's back, unable to pull him away. The woods echoed with the din.

****

The twin's shouts and Crane's screams hid the sound of the robots hastening toward them. As Kouji flung the twins off his back, Cricket and DT reached him. They lifted the wildly kicking teen from the child's body.

Kouji fought, but even with his magnified new strength, he was no match for the robots. Cricket pulled out his stun gun, subduing the teen before his frenzied punches could harm his own body. He went limp, and DT laid him on the ground. Kouji was out cold, his breathing labored.

"What do we do now?" The androids turned toward the twins.

Stunned at the violence, Tedra looked down at Kouji. "The trees," she finally ordered. "We must get him under the trees."

"Right," Gryf added. "Get him away from here. The trees will help us." How did he know that? Puzzled, Gryf looked toward the forest. Another Nacre mystery.

DT lifted Kouji while Cricket led the way to the first large tree lining the forest's edge. The teen's breathing eased for a moment, but then he began thrashing and clutching at his throat.

"This must be the virus the 'rents mentioned. Have you the antidote?" Tedra asked. At the pause, her voice grew higher. "You must have it!"

"Antidote," the robots repeated, but stood motionless. "The word is not in our memory banks."

She turned to her twin. "Gryf, what should we do?"

He spun in a circle, searching, but no one came forth to help. Even the swaying leaves had stopped their motion. "We have to try the Kiss of Life, Tedra. It's all I can think of, but there's a good chance that will work," he assured her.

She looked toward the robots. "Do you know how to administer this Kiss of Life?"

Again, they didn't move. "We were not programmed for this circumstance," squeaked Cricket.

Gazing once more at the unconscious boy, his skin bleached of all color in stark contrast to his coal black hair, Tedra bit her lip so hard, it started to bleed again. "We've got to do something. I-I guess we'll have to try it. Gryf?"

"You do it, Tedra. You're a girl."

Casting a disgusted look at her twin, Tedra dropped to her knees. Intermittent spasms overtook Kouji and he twitched. "Hold him down tight."

Cricket held the teen's head and DT his feet. Tedra leaned over him and touched her bleeding lips to his. As she forced his lips apart, the twitching stopped. Then she could no longer hear his breathing.

With a gasp, Tedra laid her ear on his chest. Over her own rapidly beating heart she caught the faint sound of air moving in and out. Once more she put her mouth on Kouji's and breathed into him. Everyone watched and waited. The tree's leaves barely fluttered. Even little Crane, thumb in his mouth, crept closer but stayed still.

"Shall we carry Kouji-san back to camp?" the

androids asked.

"It may not be safe to move him yet," Tedra said. "Let's wait a little longer."

Minutes passed. Kouji's eyelids flickered, then slowly lifted. The clouded gray hiding his pupils faded, giving way to a clear walnut brown. "Tedra?" He saw the girl first. Grimacing as he turned his aching head, Kouji caught sight of the robots and Gryf holding Crane's hand. "What happened?"

"Crane ran up the cliff, and you ran after and saved him," Gryf said. "But then you caught the virus. Space, you were scary, Kooj…"

"I caught the virus? But…but…am I okay now?"

"We think so."

"Shall we carry you back to the base?" asked Cricket, helping the teen to his feet.

"I can make it," Kouji's voice was low, uncertain. "Just let me lean on you."

"You are yourself again, Kouji-san," came DT's deep reassuring voice. Picking up Crane, the robot checked the toddler's body but found only bruises. He held the child in the crook of his elbow, while his other arm supported Kouji. Each twin held one of Cricket's hands.

"Ready?"

Kouji nodded and the tree leaves fluttered. "Yes," the twins called out. Together, they trudged through the forest to home base.

As he walked, a solemn Kouji tasted the sweet tang in the air, sniffed the rich soil he had lain on, listened to his own breathing. He glanced at the others. Crane rested his head on DT's chest, hiccupping now and again. The twins had returned to squabbling, already putting the danger behind them.

Space, but it was good to be alive!

Chapter Twenty

Stone-faced but deeply troubled, Captain Tenn stared at Kouji while a frantic Akemi ran her hands over him everywhere, checking for lesions and broken bones. "I'm okay," he protested, but didn't turn away from her touch. She kissed his scalp where a chunk of hair had been yanked out. This time he winced.

Fighting to hold back her tears, Jenny wiped Crane's runny nose, patting and petting until his sniffling stopped. Dr. Stan hurried over, shocked as he spotted the bruises on his son. "I've checked him out," Jenny assured her lifemate. "We were lucky. No broken bones, but…" She turned toward Crane and tickled his tummy, "You're going to look like a rainbow tomorrow, baby."

"Not a baby," the sniffles started again, "Caren's baby."

Jenny hugged him, careful not to squeeze the bruises. "You're right. You're my big boy."

With a nod, the doctor stepped over to Kouji, opened his bag of instruments, and gave the teen a more thorough examination. He checked his heart, his pulse, pulled down his eyelids, and inspected his eyes. Packing up his electron stethoscope, he turned to the boy. "You look good to me. How do you feel?"

"Like I'm recovering from a soccer kick to my head," Kouji replied. "Wobbly, but otherwise okay."

"You'll do." He turned to Gordon who had run up and wrapped Akemi in his arms. "Kouji just needs to rest awhile, but there's something I'd like to know. What in space did Nacre do to save him?"

"It wasn't Nacre," piped up Gryf. "Tedra gave him the Kiss of Life."

"Eeuww," muttered Kouji. "You tasted awful, Tee. Sort of metallic."

"My lip was bleeding. Kooj. That's why."

"Hmm," said Dr. Stan. "I'll need a sample of your blood, Tedra."

"You gotta take Gryf's, too!"

Gryf's yelp was squashed. "I'll take samples from all the children," the doctor said. "This is our only clue. If the cure is truly in Tedra's blood, we've made an astounding discovery." He herded the children and parents into the lab. "After I get my samples, it's off to bed, all of you." He looked up, saw Tenn standing at the back of the group, and pointed. "Captain's orders."

****

The sun rose on a perfect Nacre day. Everyone gathered in front of the lab pod where a bleary-eyed Stan reported the night's findings. "We've checked the children's samples, including baby Caren," he said. "There is an unusual component in the blood of the children who were conceived here on Nacre. It's missing from the DNA I took from Kouji. Our conclusions will need an in-depth analysis back on Earth, but it appears that when conception occurred, certain chemicals in Nacre's air united with the DNA of Crane, Caren, and the twins to create a gene resistant to the virus."

"Holy Quasars!" Lara borrowed Kouji's phrase.

"That's wonderful news."

The scientists looked at each other, huge grins breaking out. Akemi and Beyatriz opted to start a complete chemical analysis of both the blood samples and the Nacre air. Tenn clapped Stan on the back, high-fived Gordon and Dmitri. Then he hugged all the women, lingering last on Lara with a special kiss.

"Get on with it, man," Stan called as their lips lingered together.

Tenn gave him the finger and continued. "If we can isolate the gene and manufacture it chemically," he called out so all could hear, "our biggest problem with long-term settling on Nacre will be solved."

"Hooray!" the children shouted.

"Huzzah!" came DT's deep voice.

"Alakazam!" trebled Cricket.

Bey shook her head. "I will have to teach them new ways to express themselves. Maybe something in Portuguese. *Viva!*"

"Or Russian?" Dmitri said. "*Ypa!*"

"Or Japanese?" Akemi added. "*Banzai!*"

"Enough!" chorused Tenn and Lara.

"Too late—the robots have already memorized them." Kouji began to giggle.

As the euphoric couples headed back to their sleeping pods, a chorus of "*Viva! Ypa! And Banzai!*" followed in their wake.

****

"Hey, Guys, have you seen this? Hot Galaxy!"

Kouji stood at the entrance of a newly erected pod, rocking on his feet in excitement. Gryf and Tedra ran over, followed by little Crane who slipped on a stone as he hurried to catch up but forgot to cry in his anxiety to reach the children. They piled inside, calling out, poking and prodding, their shouts of glee echoing back and forth in the football field-sized space.

For the two nights the comet would pass over the planet, a special pod had been erected for the children. They exclaimed at the many holograph screens mounted in place of windows. Baby Caren's inflatable crib hung like a hammock, allowing her to view the room from a safe perch. Cricket rocked her gently while DT focused his all-seeing eyes on the others. Pizza-flavored Instapaks that heated with a touch, cookies, brownies, and iced packs of juice and soda had been supplied, to be consumed when the comet lit up the darkened sky. The children jumped and clapped when told they could stay up as late as they wished; sleeping bags had been added to the retro pajama party.

Inside the circular room were Earth's latest virtual reality helmets and shows. When they tired of that, they'd been given permission to ask Cricket and DT whatever they wanted to know. Varying degrees of crossed fingers and bitten knuckles worked their way through the adults when this was decided. Had the androids' brains developed to the point where they could outwit the precocious kids? Baiting the robots was one of their favorite games. As the adults left the pod, the last wheedle they heard was Kouji asking, "What's going on out there? You can tell me, I'm fourteen."

Akemi started to turn back, but Gordon touched her shoulder. "Don't worry," he assured her. "The robots know the score. Our kids are bright, but they've still got a way to go before they catch up with those photon-charged AI brains."

That night, the children had the time of their young lives. When they were done teasing the robots, they wore themselves out participating in VR shows and manipulating high-speed chases. In between virtual encounters, they picked out their favorite sweets and drinks. Milkyway-cola was a big favorite.

Caren and Crane fell asleep by midnight. The twins not long before dawn. The last to give in to sleep, Kouji played chess first with Cricket, then with DT. He offered a formal karate bow afterward, even calling them by their official names, R-Crick2 and R-Watson2. As he yawned and dozed off, he promised himself, *Next time I'll win.*

****

Already affected by Nacre's heightened atmosphere, the scientists relied on their robots. The children were safe, delighting in taking the first step toward growing up—an entire night without their parents. Now that they could concentrate on themselves, the four couples separated, their minds filled with fantasies of the tantalizing hours to come.

With the comet's arrival, the first night was given over to the loving trees, and to each individual's pleasure and sensual satisfaction. Familiar now, and eager for the joys to come, the couples bantered with the trees and each other as they were undressed by the questing fingerlike twigs. Then the stroking and fondling began. The thrills built. Talk sputtered to a stop, the silence broken only by shivering gasps, rapturous sighs, and long moans of delight.

Jenny and Stan, still reeling from the twin shocks of almost losing their son Crane and then finding the antidote to the virus, were engulfed in such a powerful emotional state they couldn't separate. Instead, they found an enormous tree, its broad trunk like the African baobab back on Earth. Together, they let the tree fondle them as they cherished it. Stan gazed at Jenny as she touched herself, arousing him to heights of sensitivity. The tree branches treated him to their erotic touches while he drank in the view of Jenny, one hand touching a nipple, the other separating her folds below as her branch's chocolate fingers plied their magic to her clit. The two together brought him to a phenomenal climax, but it was only the first. Sliding to the ground after she had fragmented in an incredible orgasm, Jenny bent over and drew his prick into her mouth. Her suckling combined with the twigs scratching his balls left him gasping. As he disintegrated into the shattering climax, he felt his spirit drawn from his body into hers.

Bey and Dmitri teased each other as their trees undressed them. The tasty twig fingers on the loving branches aroused them to moments of passion surpassing even their night at the hotel in Rio with its drawerful of sex toys. Velvet whips and swaying harnesses didn't compare. *Spice,* Bey thought. She was cumin in his borscht, Dmitri jalapeño in her fajita. Their trees needed no help in awakening them to a frenzy of love and commitment. Their tangy heat poured out, the taste of sex on their breath, as a whirlwind of love engulfed them.

Akemi and Gordon taught the trees and each other the most pleasing and stimulating Oriental tricks and tactics of love. Their trees were close enough for her to unwind her long black braid and let the silky hair drive him wild while the tree attended to his carnal desires. Kinky customs to arouse the male and excite the female were tried out with the help of chocolate twigs and vine-like branches. They would practice more the next night, Akemi promised, as one climax followed another until, at last, Gordon could hold back no longer and joined her. They reached the heights as one, fell apart, then felt the chocolate limbs twining them together before they slid to the ground, Gordon's wrist still wrapped around her lustrous hair.

Tenn and Lara returned to their original trees, reliving their astounding first night in the forest. All the magic returned. Lara's doubts and Tenn's decisions dissolved in the eternal mystery of their love. Hugging their tree family, they touched themselves shamelessly, watching each other in delight and sharing the thrills. Both enjoyed every minute of this night—foreplay to their coupling tomorrow.

Four pairs of lovers came together on the second night, kissing, caressing, offering tiny love bites, and licking the sensitive spots. Men and women, drunk with desire and eager to please, reveled in their partner's response to every touch. The thrills accelerated as hands, lips, and tongues moved lower and grew more inventive. The couples, each in their own circle of love, were surrounded by an enchanted circle of forest that encompassed them all.

The hours flew by, male and female reaching out to each other with total abandon. Bodies and minds linked in an intense orgy of carnal pleasure. All doubts and fears evaporated. This world, this *awakened consciousness*, offered exquisite satisfaction so perfect that only the word *enchantment* could express its heightened sensations, its ethereal yet powerful effect. Before the night was over the participants, wrapped in the dazed glow of delicious sexual release, were imprinted with infinite love.

Chapter Twenty-One

Throughout the night, the planet inoculated its citizens with Nacre's pleasures. When the comet was no more than a faint light on the horizon, however, Lara became troubled. More than troubled—her dreams still turned into invasion nightmares. Nacre was so precious. This loving, caring, uncanny planet had to be preserved. Despite the guardian drones that constantly circled her charmed world, she feared creatures in the not too distant future would figure out how to get past the barriers.

She and Tenn disagreed on what defensive measures should be taken if Nacre were threatened. Both felt strongly that their decision was the right one, and the reasons lay deep in their psyches. Lara felt the rift keenly. Why couldn't Tenn concede that for this decision she knew better? If he would only see her as an equal partner and trust her judgment, their lives on Nacre would become paradise.

She still recalled her father's words to her big brawling brothers while she, age ten, hid behind the door and eavesdropped. "Be prepared!" he roared. "Bewilder your enemy. Strike first. Never show weakness."

If all went well with this first settlement, the mother ships would arrive within the next five years, adding a thousand bodies to the population. By then the virus would be conquered and loving trees planted everywhere. She did not want to be the aggressor, but if the planet were invaded, she would fight for Nacre as a mother bear fought for her cubs. She longed for a military force trained and ready to act at a second's notice. What if the drones were somehow put out of commission? Or misdirected? What havoc would result!

Her lifemate surprised her by insisting on greeting any invaders with friendship. Without weapons. Hidden throughout the planet were protective electronic devices continually being upgraded, but the captain relied on the magic of Nacre to overcome hostility. Tenn, a Navy SEAL, for space's sake! He with a namesake poet who wrote the line that had survived through the centuries, "To strive, to seek, to find and not to yield."

Lara's body heaved with fear and frustration. She stared at the man she loved. How could he be so stubborn? So gullible? So trusting? As Tenn started to turn away, she threw a boot at him, clipping his shoulder. She wanted him to hit back, allow them to have a real fight and clear the air, but he didn't. She watched his face smooth out from its initial glower. When he was perfectly calm, he merely said, "Behave yourself. Captain's orders," and stepped out of their room.

She fell on the bunk and pounded the mattress. They had fought occasionally since their lifetime joining, but it had never been hard to kiss, compromise, and enjoy wild, make-up sex. The best kind and here on Nacre it took no effort at all. A swim in the lake, a nap under the trees, and nature would take its intoxicating course. Yet his intolerance of others' viewpoints threatened to tear them apart. She longed for the comet to return and draw out her fears. In its light, harmony glowed. Negative emotions couldn't penetrate its blanket of happiness.

****

Lara's fears of green-skinned aliens with two heads and probing tentacles never materialized. If intelligent beings coveted Nacre, she decided after some time had passed, their brains were so far advanced they would have found more compatible worlds to visit. Perhaps they even watched Earthlings from afar, contemplating their "experiment." Another line from a long-ago poem surfaced. "And that inverted bowl they call the sky…" Could it be? Were they all in a grand alien fish tank? Their emotional responses tabulated by superior creatures? What a horrid thought!

There was no use in fretting. If this planet was being used as a testing ground, as far as she was concerned Mother Nature's experiment was evolving in the right direction.

After the comet left Nacre's atmosphere, the scientists worked on designing impenetrable force fields. The captain did compromise by increasing the number and reliability of drones protecting their perimeter, while Lara helped him teach the entire community basic strategies for coping peacefully with invading species. The event that blew up their plans, however, came not from without but within.

As waves of colonists arrived within the next few years, saboteurs entered the population. Meanwhile, on the far side of Nacre's moon, a cunning trillionaire from Earth gathered and trained an invasion force of criminals and malcontents. His tight control of the

Internet and all transmissions to the media assured that no word leaked out of his grandiose plans to acquire the wealth of Nacre for himself. Believing he had convinced his well-paid saboteurs to follow his orders without question, he trained his cadre to act as the ancient Greek "Trojan Horse," dismantling the drones and other protection devices as they infiltrated the planet.

As he waited for intelligence from his advance scouts, he basked in his pomposity. But—one thing he didn't know—his spies had fallen under Nacre's spell. Great sex and a new sense of purpose left neither time nor inclination for treachery. When he received no word from his "commandos," the Manipulator didn't bother to inform his Black Ops band. Spies within were unnecessary. He would convince the dupes on Nacre that his way was the New Way, just as he had on Earth. He was invincible.

What he hadn't counted on was a flora counterattack.

Invasion Day arrived during the comet's visit five years later. The Manipulator's forces destroyed enough drones to create a wedge onto the planet. But just as they stepped onto Nacre's shore, a huge wind sprang up out of nowhere. The surprised citizens hurried into their pod suites, watching in amazement as the trees whipped into a frenzy. This had never happened before. The hurricane wind tore down the paths, blowing debris everywhere in bullet-like blasts.

The Black Ops team continued to struggle against the wind to reach the forest. As they got within range, the tree branches suddenly began to grow. Reaching out, the limbs grabbed the invaders. They surrounded them, hugged them, and bound the captives in their erotic spell.

By the time the gusting wind died down to a soft, caressing breeze, the enemies' aggression had been absorbed, along with their semen. Their clothes lay in tatters at their feet. Their weapons had been destroyed and blown into space.

In first relaxing and then exciting the prisoners, the mystical trees translated their angry emotions into explosive orgasms so overwhelming, so profound, their DNA was altered. They glanced at each other with sheepish grins, then wandered off through the forest. Eventually they climbed the cliffs and joined the new settlement, built since the virus had been conquered. With generosity a part of Nacre's charms, the newcomers were offered old clothes and invited back for the comet's visits.

Even the Manipulator experienced an erection he had thought lost to him forever. But he rejected the gift. He fought the onset of orgasm, refusing to give up control until his penis deflated like a pricked balloon. His mind cracked. Med-assist robots carried their unconscious prisoner to the psychiatric ward of their field hospital, where a distillation of tree saps salved his scratched body. When he came to, his addled brain spouted familiar phrases, but they had been scrambled into nonsense. He was returned to Earth on the next flight.

As she and Tenn helped clean up the storm's debris that had settled around their pods, Lara looked around her, still dazed by what had happened. Nacre had scored with its own defense. "This invasion has taught me something," she told her lifemate as they headed toward their new home. "We were both right."

"Yes, and you were justified." Tenn paused to wrap her in his arms, drop a kiss into her coppery hair. "It took me a long time to go beyond the authority forced on me when I turned thirteen, Lara. My father was killed, you know, and I became the emotional support of my mother and younger brother. We had a good life, but it wasn't balanced."

"That wasn't your fault."

"No, but I lost my teen years. Missed out on adolescence. I had to learn to take command just as the disturbing effects of puberty hit me. All the mental and physical changes I was undergoing were hard to cope with. When I finally got the hang of it, I couldn't let go. I had to learn anew from life's experiences, but also from you, Laralove—and you taught me a lot. Equal partners, equal shares, in all decisions."

Holding a flower he had plucked in the forest that had miraculously escaped the tempest, he brushed it across her cheeks, grinning as he watched her nostrils flare at the compelling scent—ripe peaches, brimming with sweet juices. She took the flower from him, sucking on the chocolate taste of the stem. Eyes crinkling at the sensual image, he dropped a kiss on the tip of her nose.

"I had lessons to learn, too," Lara said. "I was too intensely involved with my family, more than was healthy. I could grab their attention only through sheer force of will, often pushed in where I wasn't wanted just to belong. It didn't help, so I ran away emotionally, hid my problems in my own little cave, apart. I had to learn how to allow others in."

His gaze grew soft. "Yes, I know."

"We both had to grow, and by Space, we did! We make a good team, Admiral."

They looked up then, saw the comet, and fell under its spell. Arm in arm, they headed out to join their original crew for a night of ecstasy. All around them came moans of pleasure, sighs of contentment. Jenny and Stan floating in sweet love. Akemi and Gordon entwined. Dmitri and Bey skydiving into the fall.

Lara and Tenn attached themselves to the others and plunged through waves of enchantment to reach the glowing promise on the distant shore. Spiritual satisfaction joined sexual satiation to reach Nirvana. Tingling, lingering happiness. Bliss. It was a promise only hinted at when they first noticed the many colored leaves waving to them as they hurtled toward an unknown world. So many years ago... Nacre had indeed lived up to its essence of pure pearl. Surely their planet was unique in the universe.

****

As the settlers of Nacre enjoyed a night of blissful carnal connection, the comet flew by. The invasion and the incredible storm that followed had sent up shock waves, knocking it one degree out of orbit. It continued on, the icy stream of its tail flying at last over a distant planet, the third revolving around another sun. There it collided with space debris thrown off by that world. A small piece of its tail dropped off, showering meteorites onto the land below. Within the rocks that fell, packed tightly and suspended in water droplets, billions of pheromones collided. And waited...

About the Author

I fell in love with the sky when I moved out West. Tiny pinpricks of light from a trillion galaxies in uncountable universes pierce the black velvet and enchant me. By day I'm surrounded by fantastic, ever-changing clouds that shape my imagination beneath a backdrop of brilliant blue. From here I can write, read, run, join friends, watch TV, eat funky meals, and set off for foreign parts, always to return.

~*~

I love to hear from my readers at
veebentleypinch@gmail.com.

~*~

To chat with Vee and other Wild Rose Press authors of erotic romance, join us at
www.groups.yahoo.com/group/thewilderroses.

Also Available

Peril, Passion, Peru

by

Eve Dew Crook

http://a.co/9qUyFNm

Pursuit and passion, bullets and blowguns, arousing art and sublime satisfaction—welcome to Peru.

When her husband walks out leaving their final divorce papers unsigned, bilingual editor Jill Flanders hops on a plane to Peru to find him. She's waited a long time to be rid of the lying coward and refuses to lose her chance at a fulfilling life.

In Peru, she meets Dex Conroy, a ceramics specialist hot on her ex-husband's trail after precious artifacts go missing. Jill is disturbed by her instant attraction to Dex. Nevertheless, she joins him in search of the missing man and vanished treasure.

As the hunt heats up, the hesitant relationship between Jill and Dex blossoms. Can the newly awakened lovers find what their hearts seek while accidents accrue and poisoned blowgun darts start flying?

Also Read

Universe Hunters: Taken

by

C.L. Scholey

http://a.co/6YnStQY

Being lost in the forest is the least of Cali's worries when she's attacked by flesh-eating creature not of this world. She is rescued by a scorching alien light that kills the creature but inadvertently burns her. Cali wakes to find her body healed but her sanity in question. She can't really be zipping through space on a vessel manned by two light beings who have taken the form of human men—two sexy as hell human men calling themselves…Universe Hunters.

Two male beings, one human female. Life as Cali knows it changes in the blink of an eye, or in her case, a flicker of light.

Thank you for purchasing this
publication of The Wild Rose Press, Inc.
If you enjoyed the story, we would appreciate
your letting others know by leaving a review.
For other wonderful stories, please visit our
on-line bookstore at www.wilderroses.com.

For questions or more
information contact us at
info@thewildrosepress.com.

The Wild Rose Press, Inc.
www.thewilderroses.com

Stay current with The Wild Rose Press, Inc.
Like us on Facebook
https://www.facebook.com/TheWildRosePress
And Follow us on Twitter
https://twitter.com/WildRosePress

www.ingramcontent.com/pod-product-compliance
Lightning Source LLC
Chambersburg PA
CBHW072150170626
46813CB00004BA/1749